D1604423

J. T. EDSON'S
FLOATING OUTFIT

The toughest bunch of Rebels that ever lost a war, they fought for the South, and then for Texas, as the legendary Floating Outfit of "Ole Devil" Hardin's O.D. Connected ranch.

MARC COUNTER was the best-dressed man in the West: always dressed fit-to-kill. BELLE BOYD was as deadly as she was beautiful, with a "Manhattan" model Colt tucked under her long skirts. THE YSABEL KID was Comanche fast and Texas tough. And the most famous of them all was DUSTY FOG, the ex-cavalryman known as the Rio Hondo Gun Wizard.

J. T. Edson has captured all the excitement and adventure of the raw frontier in this magnificent Western series. Turn the page for a complete list of Berkley Floating Outfit titles.

J. T. EDSON'S
FLOATING OUTFIT
WESTERN ADVENTURES
FROM BERKLEY

J.T. Edson

THE SOUTH WILL RISE AGAIN

A BERKLEY BOOK
published by
BERKLEY PUBLISHING CORPORATION

This Berkley book contains the complete
text of the original edition.
It has been completely reset in a type face
designed for easy reading, and was printed
from new film.

THE SOUTH WILL RISE AGAIN

A Berkley Book / published by arrangement with
Transworld Publishers, Ltd.

PRINTING HISTORY
Corgi edition published 1972
Berkley edition / March 1980

ISBN: 0–425–04491–2

A BERKLEY BOOK® TM 757,375
Berkley Books are published by Berkley Publishing Corporation,
200 Madison Avenue, New York, New York 10016.
PRINTED IN THE UNITED STATES OF AMERICA

*For my bueno amigo Louis Masterson
in the hope that he will give Morgan
Kane a decent gun.*

CHAPTER ONE

Death to All Traitors

The sign at the side of the stage read, 'MELANIE BEAUCHAMPAINE & TEXAS, Cowgirl Magic'.

There were few male members of the audience who would have objected to sharing their camp-fires with such 'cowgirls'. Each wore a skin-tight, sleeveless, black satin blouse of *extremely* extreme décolleté, ending short enough to leave its wearer's midriff exposed. The riding breeches, of the same glossy material, clung so snugly that every curve, depression and movement of the hips, buttocks, thighs and calves showed tantalizingly. They had black Stetsons set at jaunty angles on their heads. Hessian riding boots graced their feet. Each had on a gunbelt, with a revolver in its holster.

Of equal height, Melanie Beauchampaine was a tall, slender girl; although anything but flat-chested, skinny or boyish in appearance. For all that, she was out-done in the matter of a figure by the rich, voluptuous curves of her beautiful assistant. A close observer might have noticed that Texas's left eye was blackened and Melanie had a thickened top lip, hinting possibly at a disagreement between them over some matter.

Whatever the cause of controversy had been, the girls displayed no sign of it. They were a trifle nervous, but that might have been on account of the quality of certain members of their audience. The Variety Theatre in San Antonio de Bexar was that night acting as host to the Governor of Texas, Stanton Howard, and several prominent figures in the State's all-important cattle industry.

Nervous or not, the girls had given a good performance of magical tricks. They had been a fitting climax to a pleasant show. Clearly, however, they were coming to the end of their act.

'And now I would like the assistance of a few gentlemen,' Melanie announced. Seeing several male members of the audience rise hurriedly, she went on: 'With so many handsome volunteers to choose from, I do declare I don't know who to take.'

'We'd best pick them quickly, Melanie,' Texas suggested, speaking in a similar Southern drawl to that of her companion. 'If we don't, they'll stompede all over us.'

'Why sure,' Melanie agreed. 'Let's be tactful for once, shall we? I think all you boys had better sit down and we'll get somebody a bit further away. They won't be coming on the stage, anyways.' Waiting until the men had returned to their seats, she waved a hand towards the guests-of-honor's box. 'Perhaps his Honor, the Governor, will oblige?'

'I wish I was the Governor,' helled one of the disappointed candidates.

'The job has to have *some* consolations,' Governor Howard pointed out, standing up.

'May I ask Captain Dusty Fog to take part,' Melanie called, 'without being thought to be making favorites?'

'Go on, Dusty,' the burly rancher known as Shanghai Pierce suggested. 'It'll make up for you losing out on that beef contract.'

'We haven't lost it yet,' the well-dressed young man whom the rancher had addressed replied and came to his feet.

'No bickering, boys!' Melanie warned. 'This is a peace conference you're all here for.' Swinging towards the box on the opposite side of the theatre, in which were seated the same ranchers' foremen, she said, 'Now let me see, how about you, Mr. Figert?'

"Which shows you've got right good taste as well as beauty, ma'am,' drawled Miffin Kennedy's segundo as he stood up.

'If I get something like that said to me, I'm picking the next one,' Texas declared. 'Mr. Counter, will you make our other assistant?'

'Why I'd admire to assist you, most any old time, ma'am,' declared the handsome blond giant to whom the words had been directed.

Going by the glance Melanie threw at her assistant, she had not expected the interruption. However, she made no comment on it.

'Now Texas will go into the magic box,' Melanie announced, indicating the large, gaily-painted but as yet unused structure standing in the center of the stage. 'We will see what happens next.'

'Mind you-all drop me on top of the handsomest of them, Melanie,' Texas requested, opening the door and showing the empty interior of the box, then entering.

'Why I'd do that, honey,' Melanie answered, closing the door. 'But I doubt if Governor Stanton's wife would approve.'

There was a laugh from the audience, wiped away by the orchestra in the pit commencing a long roll of the drums.

Every eye was on the slender, beautiful girl as she reached for and jerked open the door of the box.

It was not empty!

Two male figures in range clothes sprang out, holding revolvers.

'Death to all traitors!' bellowed the smaller, swinging his weapon into alignment.

Shots thundered from both the newcomers' revolvers, their barrels pointing towards the guests-of-honor's box. Clapping his hands to his forehead, Governor Howard spun around and tumbled to the floor. Clutching at his left breast, Captain Dusty Fog was pitched backwards and landed across the knees of Pierce and the third rancher, Richard King.

Instantly wild confusion reigned in the building. Due

to the delicate nature of the situation—the Governor was trying to avert a range war between his companions—the San Antonio town marshal had caused every visitor to the theatre to be disarmed on arrival. Voices raised in shouts. Women screamed. Men rose, grabbing at empty holsters and blocking the lines of fire of the peace officers who were standing guard at the exits.

The moment the two men had made their appearance, Melanie stepped into the back of the box. She pressed herself to the rear, for there was little enough room inside.

Having fired at and sent the Governor down, the smaller of the pair leapt to Melanie's side. Instead of following them immediately, the taller, younger man—a boy in his late teens—swiveled in the direction of the foremen's box. Left, right, left, the long-barreled 1860 Army Colts in his hands boomed out. Mark Counter's giant frame rocked under the impact. Before the big blond had pitched head-long out of sight, the youngster was joining his companion and the girl. The bottom of the box sank rapidly downwards and carried them from view.

CHAPTER TWO

You're Not Long Out of Jail

A few weeks before the incident at the Variety Theatre.

Strolling slowly along the sidewalk in the direction of the German's Hotel at Mooringsport, Sabot the Mysterious displayed the attitude of a man engrossed in his problems. He was so preoccupied with his thoughts that he ignored the scrutiny of the slender, beautiful young woman who was standing outside Klein's General Store. Somewhat over-painted and dressed in the kind of clothes poorer actresses, or saloongirls, wore when traveling between jobs or walking the streets, she held the inevitable parasol and vanity bag in her left hand.

Going closer, Sabot became *very* aware of the girl. Advancing in a casual-appearing manner, she bumped into him. The collision was anything but accidental. As soon as their bodies came into contact, her right hand slipped under his jacket towards the wallet in its inside pocket.

Sabot had just concluded a most satisfactory interview with the town's marshal and was returning to his hotel feeling, for the first time in days, a sense of relief. The state of nervous tension under which he had been living since arriving in Shreveport, to fulfil an engagement at the Grand Palace Theatre, was ebbing away.

Give de Richelieu his due, Sabot mused before coming into contact with the girl, he had been correct in

5

his assessment of how the military and civil authorities
would react if their enterprise had not reached its
ultimate aims. For all that, being aware that things *had*
gone wrong, the business in which they had been
engaged was of such a serious nature Sabot had hardly
been left feeling comfortable, or easy in his mind.

Nobody could have been relaxed and free from care
when trying to stir up an open rebellion against the
United States Congress. Which is what Sabot the
Mysterious and the other members of the Brotherhood
For Southron Freedom had been hoping to do in
Shreveport.

When the Brotherhood had got into their stride, with
a campaign of agitation that was calculated to provoke
the Southern States into a second attempt to secede
from the Union, they had met with little success. By
1874, the worst elements and excesses of Reconstruction
had been eliminated. Prosperity was returning to the
lands south of the Mason-Dixon line and the white
population had no desire for a resumption of the hard-
ships of war, nor to sample again the bitter consequences of defeat.

There had been some response to the Brotherhood's
rallying cries; 'Give money to buy arms!'; 'Make ready
for the day of reckoning with the Yankees!'; 'THE
SOUTH WILL RISE AGAIN!'. Not enough, however,
to have made the dreams of secession become a reality.
The men behind the conspiracy had realized that some
dramatic proof of the Union's perfidy and hatred of the
South was needed. So a devilish plot had been hatched
to bring this about.

All that had been achieved so far was to obtain sufficient money to buy a hundred obsolete Henry
repeating rifles and ten thousand rounds of .44/28 Tyler
B. Henry ammunition. The chief satisfaction from the
purchase had been that the arms—and some military
uniforms and accoutrements taken as an excuse for
making it—had originally been destined to equip a
Kansas volunteer Dragoon regiment that was being
raised to fight the Confederate States. So far, the

weapons had not been put to use in the cause of Southern freedom.

They would have been, if everything had gone according to plan in Shreveport.

Although friendly relations had been resumed between the United States Army and the Southern civilian population through much of Dixie, that happy state had not existed in Shreveport. Brevet Lieutenant Colonel Szigo, in command of the local Army post, was an embittered man who had been passed over for promotion or even elevation from his substantive rank of captain. Blaming the South, which had given up the fight before his brevet rank could be made substantive, he had allowed—even overtly encouraged—his men to behave as if they were still a garrison force of the Reconstruction Period. So there had been little love lost between the soldiers and the citizens.

Knowing of the hostility which existed in Shreveport, the leaders of the Brotherhood had selected it as the ideal area for their demonstration. Having thrown the United States Secret Service off the trail of the arms,* they had made ready for action.

Throughout his engagement at the Grand Palace Theatre, Sabot had worked to win the confidence of the Army officers at the post and certain influential members of Shreveport society. He had succeeded to such an extent that Szigo not only permitted him to give a benefit performance free to ex-members of the Confederate States Army and Navy—he had already done the same for the soldiers—but had agreed, in the interests of avoiding possible clashes, to place the town off limits to his own troops on the evening of the show.

That latter, engineered by Sabot, had been very necessary to the success of the scheme.

Towards the end of the benefit, masked members of the Brotherhood had 'invaded' the stage and 'interrupted' Sabot's display of magical illusions. They had made inflammatory speeches, then taken certain

* Told in: *TO ARMS! TO ARMS, IN DIXIE!*

precautions to ensure that nobody interfered with their escape.

Present in the audience had been Colonel Alburgh Winslow, a member of the Louisiana State Legislature and owner of the *Shreveport Herald-Times,* and other prominent citizens noted for their moderate opinions and their efforts to prevent open conflict between the townspeople and the soldiers. It had been planned that, later in the evening—disguised in the Dragoons' uniforms*—Victor Brandt would take an 'escort' and 'arrest' Winslow's party on charges of organizing a treasonable assembly. Any who had resisted were to be shot on the spot. Those who had gone quietly would have been murdered and their bodies—decorated with boards inscribed, 'So perish all traitors to the Union'—left hanging in the city's main square.

Unfortunately, Sabot's assistant, Princess Selima Baba, had not been convincing in her behavior during the 'invasion' of the stage. In fact, her attitude had threatened to spoil the whole effect. So, in the dressing-rooms after changing into his uniform, Brandt—an arrogant, bad-tempered and vicious young man—had beaten her with his fists. Furious at the punishment, Selima had fled. Suspecting that she might warn the authorities of what was planned, Sabot had suggested that the scheme be delayed until she had been captured. Taking two of his men, Brandt had set off to fetch the girl back. One of his escort had returned to say that she was trying to reach Colonel Szigo, but that the others were on her trail and hoped to prevent her visiting the Army post. Brandt had also warned that the 'arrests' must not be attempted until he had given the word. As he alone wore an officer's uniform, that had been sound advice. The party would have lacked credibility if it had arrived to make the arrests comprising only enlisted men.

When Brandt and his companion had not returned in a reasonable time, Sabot had taken it upon himself to

* By 1863, the Dragoons had begun to wear the standard U.S. Cavalry uniform.

call off the whole affair. Dismissing the men, he had
sent a warning to de Richelieu—who had left the theatre
to supervise the delivery of the arms from their hiding
place five miles away—that something was wrong. After
that, Sabot had continued with his pre-arranged intention of leaving Shreveport on the *Texarkana Belle*
and traveling to Mooringsport. From the town, he was
to commence an itinerary of Texas engagements.
During it, he was to spread the word of the 'Yankees'
dastardly deed and to help arouse enmity in the Lone
Star State.

On his arrival in Mooringsport, shortly before noon,
Sabot had immediately visited the town's marshal. He
had told the peace officer a story that would, all being
well, hold water when compared with the recollections
of the audience concerning what had happened on the
stage.

To hear Sabot tell it, he had been attacked and, along
with Selima, driven to his dressing-room by the masked
agitators. After they had completed their treasonable
activities, he had been compelled to return to the stage
and satisfy the audience that he had not been harmed.
Then his assailants had departed, taking Selima as a
hostage against is behavior. They had also warned that
he would be kept under observation and killed, along
with the girl, if he should attempt to consult the
authorities.

Fearing for his assistant's life, despite the men's
promise that she would be allowed to join him aboard
the *Texarkana Belle,* Sabot had complied with their
demands. However, the girl had not made her appearance at sailing time and he had left without her. In
exculpation for his desertion, he had claimed that, on
thinking the matter over, he had reached the conclusion
that Selina had been an active participant in the plot.
That, he had told the marshal, explained how the
masked men had known the trick with which he planned
to end his show; and had been able to substitute their
treasonable portraits—which portrayed Union generals
in an uncomplimentary light and showed an unsavory

aspect of life under Reconstruction—for the harmless illustrations which he would have used.

Although the marshal had apparently been satisfied with Sabot's story, he had insisted that the magician remain in Mooringsport until after he had telegraphed the Shreveport authorities. Stating that he had intended staying over to give a few performances, Sabot had acceded to the request. He had been allowed to go about his business and was promised that he would be kept informed of any future developments.

At four o'clock in the afternoon, a deputy had arrived at the hotel and asked the magician to accompany him to the marshal's office. Managing to conceal his anxiety, Sabot had obeyed. He had spent the hours in trepidation, wondering what the answer from Shreveport would be. Flight had been impossible, for it would have been construed as evidence of guilt. The marshal's kindly, sympathetic attitude had hinted that he had nothing to fear.

There had been answers from the Shreveport Police Department and the commanding officer of the Army post. The former had merely stated that the incident at the theatre was being investigated, but everything pointed to Sabot being a victim rather than a participant. Numerous witnesses had seen him struck down and had testified to the interruption to his performance.

The latter message had been both puzzling and a source of relief. Apparently Selima had 'escaped from her captors', but was killed before she could reach the gates of the post. Opening fire, the guard had shot down her murderers—there was no mention of them having been in uniform—before they could flee from the scene of the crime.

The puzzling aspect had been that the message was signed, 'Manderley' and not 'Szigo'.

With something like satisfaction, the marshal had said that the intruders had slipped through the Shreveport police's and the Army's fingers. Sabot was free to go. The meeting had ended amicably with the magician handing out free tickets to his first performance.

Sabot had quit the marshal's office with a lighter heart than when he had entered. Despite the failure to carry out de Richelieu's scheme, the affair had not ended too badly for him. He had emerged without being suspected of complicity in the plot. With Brandt dead, he stood a chance of stepping into the 'captain's'—Brandt's rank for the deception—shoes as second-in-command of the Brotherhood. Not that he gave a damn for the ideals which guided de Richelieu's actions. He merely wanted to gain a larger proportion of the financial benefits he felt sure would accrue as a result of the organization's activities.

Thinking of the future had brought another aspect to Sabot's attention. He would be continuing to produce his show, which allowed members of the Brotherhood to visit, or meet in, different towns without raising questions concerning their presence. So he would require a replacement for Selima. Only this time he must be more selective in his choice. His rivals for Brandt's position might use Selima's inadequacies as a tool against him, blaming him for the failure of the Shreveport affair.

What Sabot needed was a pretty, shapely, fairly intelligent girl who was not overburdened by scruples. There had not seemed much chance of him finding such a person in the small Lake Caddo town of Mooringsport.

Having just reached that conclusion, Sabot collided with the girl and felt her fingers reaching into his jacket. He grinned internally at her mistake. Of course, if he had been wearing his stage make-up and clothes, instead of being clean-shaven and clad in a snappy gray suit of the latest Eastern sports fashion, she might have known better than to make the attempt at picking his pocket.

Catching hold of the girl's wrist, before she could completely withdraw the wallet from his pocket, the magician plucked her hand from beneath his jacket.

They had that particular length of the sidewalk to themselves and he realized how nobody could see what was happening between them.

'Let me go!' the girl hissed, trying to snatch her wrist from his grasp. 'What do you-all think you're doing?'

Sabot was on the point of shouting for somebody to fetch the marshal. Hearing the girl speak, he hurriedly revised his opinion and studied her. The ribbons of a grubby white spoon bonnet were fastened in a bow under the chin of a beautiful face. The hat effectively covered her hair, but Sabot sensed that it had been cut almost boyishly short. Taken with the tanned texture of her skin, the hair's length was significant. She had on a basque jacket, but did not wear the socially-required blouse underneath it, and a shiny black skirt which emphasized the shape of her slender hips before ending short enough to expose an indecorous amount of her cheap high-buttoned shoes.

While her appearance had intimated that she was a not-too-prominent actress or a saloongirl, she had spoken in the accent of a well-raised Southern lady. Except that her tones had been hardened and harshened by life and unpleasant experiences. Such a combination suggested possibilities to the magician.

'Shall we call the marshal so that you can complain?' Sabot inquired, holding the girl close to him with his left hand while the right moved swiftly on a mission which she failed to detect. 'I'll do it, if you're so inclined.'

'So call him and we'll see whose word he'll take,' challenged the girl, drawing back but still held by the wrist.

For all her brash answer, she looked decidedly uneasy.

'Very well,' countered the magician and turned his head as if to do so.

'This is all a misunderstanding,' the girl put in hurriedly. 'I don't want to be involved in a public spectacle. So I'll overlook your behavior.'

Retaining his grip on her wrist, Sabot moved back to arm's length and gave her another scrutiny. While

slender and willowly, she was anything but scraggy.
Dressed in a suitable manner, she would be worth
looking at. Despite her obvious poverty, she carried herself with an air of breeding and refinement. That was
possible. Reconstruction had seen many formerly well-
to-do and respectable Southern girls driven on to the
stage, or into even less savory occupations. Most of the
unfortunates blamed the Yankees bitterly for their
downfalls and had no love for supporters of the Union.
Some could not adjust to their lowered status. Those
who did, in Sabot's experience, became tough, hard and
unscrupulous.

Unless the magician missed his guess, the would-be
pickpocket fell into that category.

Moreover, there were certain indications about her as
to where she had spent time recently.

'Don't try and run away!' the magician warned,
releasing her. 'If you do, I'll have you arrested. You
wouldn't like that. You're not long out of jail, are you?'

'How dare you?' the girl spat, with well-simulated indignation. 'Just what do you mean by——'

'That spoon bonnet looks like hell on you, but you
have to wear it to hide your hair,' Sabot interrupted and
grinned as her right hand fluttered nervously towards
her head. 'They cut women prisoners' hair short at the
State Penitentiary. Your clothing suggests that you're
an actress, or a calico cat. But you've got a tan that says
you've spent more time out of doors than you would in
either job. It all adds up to you just having been released
from prison.'

'Smart, aren't you?' the girl demanded bitterly.

'Shrewd—and correct.'

'All right, mister. So I've only been out for a few
days. What's that got to do with you?'

'I could have you sent back,' Sabot warned her.

'For what?'

'Stealing my wallet.'

'Try proving that n——' grinned the girl.

'Before you make me do that,' Sabot answered, 'take
a look in your vanity bag.''

Jerking open the mouth of the bag, the girl glanced inside with an attitude of disbelief. Then she stiffened and stared harder. Raising her eyes, she glared at Sabot in open-mouthed amazement.

'I-It's there!' the girl croaked, looking frightened. 'What——How——?'

'The next time you try to pick a pocket, make sure it's not a magician's,' Sabot advised. 'Like I said, I could send you back to jail.'

'But you won't if I'm nice to you, huh?' the girl guessed.

'Not entirely. I assume that you're short of money.'

'Mister, that's a mighty shrewd assumption.'

'Could you use a meal?'

'I aimed to buy one with whatever I found in your wallet,' the girl admitted. 'The food at those stagecoach way stations isn't fit for a hawg, or a Yankee. In that order.'

'If you'll be my guest,' the magician said, delighted that he had summed up another aspect of her character so well. She had no love for 'Yankees'. 'I'll stand treat for a meal.'

'As a reward for me trying to lift your leather?' the girl said dryly.

'Do you want the meal, or don't you?'

'I want it. But I was wondering why you're being so all-fired nice to me.'

'Why do you think I am?'

'If it's for the reason I suspect, you're wasting your time,' the girl declared. 'One of the reasons I'm so short of money is that I don't.''

'I'll remember that, if I get inclined to want it,' Sabot promised. 'My last assistant quit and I need a good-looking, shapely girl to replace her. While we're eating, I'll decide whether to offer you the job or not.'

'Why, thank you ''most to death,'' ' replied the girl, taking the wallet from her bag and handing it back to its owner. 'And I'll decide whether I want to take it.'

CHAPTER THREE

Stomp the Bastard Good

Although Sabot the Mysterious did not realize it, he had played into the hands of the Brotherhood For Southron Freedom's most implacable and deadly enemy.

Yet, taking her early life into consideration, Belle Boyd might have seemed ideally suited to become a leading light in an attempt to secede from the Union.

Born the only child of a wealthy Baton Royale plantation owner, Belle had been given a most unconventional upbringing. In addition to receiving the normal instruction in the social and ladylike graces, she had been taught to ride astride, fence with sabre or epee, handle every type of firearm and perform skilfully at savate, the foot and fist boxing practiced by the French Creoles. Her father had always wanted a son and, by teaching her the martial arts, had given her an excellent education for what had lay ahead.

Shortly before the War Between the States had commenced, a drunken mob of pro-Unionist fanatics—led by a pair of liberal-intellectuals called Tollinger and Barmain—had raided the Boyds' plantation. By the time the family's 'downtrodden and abused' slaves had driven off the attackers, Belle was wounded, her parents dead, and the fine old Boyd mansion had been reduced to a blazing ruin.

On her recovery, Belle had sworn to take revenge on Tollinger and Barmain. They had fled to Union territory and were said to be members of the United States Secret Service. As an aid to hunting them, Belle

had joined a Confederate spy ring organized by her
cousin, Rose Greenhow. Acting as a courier, the girl
had specialized in delivering messages and other information through the enemy's lines. Gaining fame for
such work, she had graduated to handling assignments
of a difficult, dangerous nature.* To the Yankees, for
whom she had become a thorn in the flesh, she had
earned the title, the Rebel Spy.

Not until the War was over had Belle's path crossed
that of her quarry. In pursuing and settling her account
with them, she had paved the way for a change in her
employers, if not in her way of life.† She had sworn the
oath of allegiance to the Union and accepted General
Handiman's offer to become a member of the United
States Secret Service.

Called in by the head of her organization to help
prevent the Henry rifles from being delivered, Belle
might have been faced by a clash of loyalties when she
had learned of the Brotherhood For Southron Freedom.
It did not arise. One of the organization's leaders,
whom she knew only as 'the Frenchman', had been
responsible for the death of two of her friends. He had
tortured and brutally killed Madame Lucienne with his
own hands. So Belle had sworn that she would take
revenge on him, even if she had to smash the
Brotherhood to do it.

It had been chiefly due to Belle Boyd's efforts that the
Shreveport affair had failed. Arriving in that city, with
information that something special was planned at the
theatre, she had been a member of the audience. In fact,
disguised as an elderly woman, she had been on the
stage as part of Sabot's committee.

A variety of circumstances had led her to deduce the
nature of the plan's second phase. Brandt and his companion had died at her hand, inside the Army post, after
they had murdered Selima.

Unknown to the Brotherhood, there had been a

* Told in: *THE COLT AND THE SABRE, THE REBEL SPY* and
THE BLOODY BORDER.

† Told in: *BACK TO THE BLOODY BORDER.*

change of command at the camp. Stories of Szigo's treatment of the Shreveport citizens had reached Washington. To avoid trouble, a more moderate commanding officer had been dispatched secretly to take charge and bring an improvement in the relations between the soldiers and the townspeople.

Having failed to arrest any of the Brotherhood, Colonel Manderley and Belle had debated their next line of action. One point had been decided upon. Under no circumstances must the full implications of the plot be made public. To have done so would have come close to achieving the Brotherhood's ends for them.

Naturally the incident at the theatre could not be overlooked. However, Colonel Winslow was Belle's uncle and he had agreed that his newspaper would treat the affair as nothing more than a stupid, ill-advised piece of foolishness. Shown in such a light, it would soon be forgotten. Winslow had also arranged for a story which would explain away Selima's murder and the deaths of the two conspirators.

Writing a report of her activities, Belle had arranged for it to be delivered at all speed to her superiors in New Orleans. Then she had made her preparations for resuming her pursuit of the Frenchman. Having arrived in Shreveport expecting trouble, she had brought in her trunk a number of items which she had felt might be of use. Selecting clothing that she believed would suit the situation, she had asked her uncle to hold the rest of her property until she could let him know where to send it. Then she had organized transport for the journey.

It had been decided that Sabot offered the best means of locating the rest of the Brotherhood. Following him had proved to be the easiest part of the affair. To help police the Red River, the U.S. Navy had placed two of its fast steam launches at the Army's disposal. So Belle had not needed to wait for a regular passenger boat, but had traveled from Shreveport in a launch. In that way, she had arrived in Mooringsport at three o'clock in the afternoon. She had taken a room in the town's cheapest hotel, then set off to locate the magician. Finding his place of residence had not been difficult. Having learnt that he was paying a visit to the marshal's office, she had waited with the intention of scraping up an acquaintance.

After the trouble Selima had caused, Belle had suspected that the magician might be looking for a more reliable type of assistant. She had settled upon a character which she believed would satisfy his requirements and had made the correct decision.

Over a meal at the German's Hotel, Belle had told Sabot how she had been put in jail for helping to swindle 'a fat Yankee pig who deserved it'. She had also admitted that the Pinkerton National Detective Agency was looking for her. Not for any serious crime, or with extra persistence, but merely because they liked to solve their cases and she could help with one. She had declared that, having made alterations to her appearance, they would be unlikely to recognize her. All in all, she had left the magician with the impression that she was a tough, unscrupulous girl, with a deep, lasting hatred for anybody who lived north of the Mason-Dixon line. He had accepted that she had once been rich, but was left a pauper by the War and had lived a hard life since its end.

Satisfied that he had found a suitable candidate for the post, Sabot had offered to make her his assistant. After haggling over pay, Belle had accepted. She had said that her name was 'Melanie Beauchampaine', but would not object to being known as Princess Selima Baba.

The rest of the day, Belle had never been out of Sabot's sight for more than a few minutes. She had tried on the garments which she would wear on the stage. Flimsy, scanty and revealing, they were what people expected of a girl who had been 'rescued from a life of sin in the Sultan of Tripoli's harem'. They had required some alterations, for the previous Selima had been a more buxom girl. That had been done and Belle had spent the evening learning her duties.

While Sabot had apparently trusted her, he had

pumped her for more details about her past. She had
told him plenty, hinting that she had double-crossed
confederates and generally conveying the impression
that she would not be troubled by scruples.

One factor more than any other had helped Belle to
gain acceptance and avoid arousing suspicion. Mooringsport lay on the shore of Lake Caddo. To reach it,
one had to branch away from the Red River along the
Caddo River. Only one boat made regular runs between
the town and Shreveport. As the girl had not been on
the *Texarkana Belle*, Sabot accepted that she must have
either come in on a stagecoach from the west, or had
been in Mooringsport before he had arrived. He did not
suspect that she had found another means of traversing
the distance.

Belle had learned her duties well enough to help in
Sabot's first performance. It had been a novel, not entirely pleasant, sensation, appearing on the stage clad in
the flimsy, revealing 'harem girl's' costume; but she had
forced herself to go through with the act. She had
known that she would soon become accustomed to the
situation.

One thing Belle had established quickly was that she
wanted no amatory relationships with her fellow performers. Sabot, the five members of the orchestra and
the two cross-talk comedians had accepted her decision
without question. Not so the show's baritone, who
fancied himself as being something of a lady-killer. It
had taken Belle's knee, delivered hard into his groin, to
convince him that when she said 'no', that was exactly
what she meant. Sensing that he had found an ideal
assistant, Sabot had backed up Belle in her treatment of
the singer. The magician had issued a warning to all his
employees, after the incident, that 'Melanie's' wishes
must be respected.

Being only a small town, Mooringsport could not
support a theatre. So the show had taken place on an
improvised stage in the biggest saloon. While they had
had a good reception each night, Belle wondered how
Sabot was able to afford to play to such a restricted

audience. He seemed content to do so and she did not ask questions.

Four days went by and on the fifth evening, Belle was presented with an opportunity to impress Sabot.

During the magician's performance, the girl had seen what she suspected was an exchange of signals between the magician and a big, burly, red-haired man in the audience. Although the latter was dressed differently, Belle had recognized him as 'Mick', a member of the Brotherhood whom she had seen in Memphis. Apart from the brief byplay, Sabot gave no further sign of interest in Mick.

After the show was over, and the girl had donned her street clothes in the small store-room which had been converted into her dressing-room, she went to find her employer. All the rest of the cast had already gone, but the door of the men's dressing-room was open. Seated at the table, with his 'jewel'-emblazoned turban, black opera cloak and frock coat removed, the magician was peeling off his false moustachios and sharp-pointed chin beard. At his side, the owner of the saloon had just finished counting out a pile of money.

'I'm sorry it's not more, Sabot,' the owner was saying. 'You've given me a full house and good bar sales every night. I'm sorry to see you go.'

'I've other commitments, unfortunately,' Sabot answered, his sallow face almost looking as if it was unfortunate. 'And this's enough. We couldn't move on until the *Belle* came back and doing the shows had helped me to teach Melanie her duties.'

'Say!' the owner ejaculated, indicating the newspaper which lay on the dressing-table. 'It was a bad thing, your other gal getting killed that way.'

'Tragic,' Sabot intoned soberly. 'It seems I misjudged her and she wasn't in cahoots with those men. She escaped and was trying to notify the authorities. If she had only come to me, things would have been different.'

'Maybe she didn't get away from the bastards until after the *Belle*'d pulled out,' the owner consoled.

'Anyways, it's not *you* us folks blames for her getting killed.'

There had been considerable discussion caused by the reports of the 'mysterious doings' in Shreveport. Some of the *Texarkana Belle*'s officers had been at the show. They, and the marshal, had told enough of Sabot's part in the affair for a garbled version of it to have made the rounds. Belle had watched and listened, hoping to learn in which direction public sentiment was swinging. From her findings, she had concluded that the officially-sponsored version of Selima's murder had swung public sympathy away from the Brotherhood. If the people of Mooringsport reflected the trend throughout the South, Sabot and his companions would be unable to benefit in any way from the incident.

'She was a good girl,' Sabot sighed, 'but always chasing after men. That's one problem I don't have to worry about now. Not chasing after m——.'

'Hey, Selima!' called the owner, becoming aware of Belle's presence and wanting to warn the magician before he made an indiscreet statement concerning his assistant's sexual behaviour.

'Changed and ready already, heh?' Sabot went on, turning to look at the girl. 'Come in. I'll not be long. Then we'll go back to the hotel and it'll be pay day.'

'There's a word I love to hear,' Belle smiled, advancing. Then the newspaper's headlines caught her eye. 'Hey! Do you know her? Of course you do. I'm sorry, Sabby.'

Acting contrite and flustered, as a person would after making such a mistake, Belle picked up the paper. To the men, it seemed that she was merely covering her embarrassment; or motivated by morbid curiosity concerning her predecessor's death.

Under the headline, 'MAGICIAN'S ASSISTANT MURDERED', the *Shreveport Herald-Times* had done a fine job in covering the true facts of Selima's death. Her uncle had used it in a masterly fashion to condemn the Brotherhood's activities. Dismissing the incident at the theatre as he had promised, he had also commented that what had probably begun as a practical joke misfired badly when Selima had escaped. Being a courageous young lady with a strong sense of public spirit, she must have intended to report the incident to the authorities. Rather than allow it, the men had pursued her and killed her within sight of the post's main entrance. Unfortunately for the murderers, the guards had been on the alert and both men had been shot down while resisting arrest. There was no mention, once more, of Brandt and his companion having been dressed in U.S. Army uniforms.

A second headline announced Lieutenant Colonel Szigo's departure 'for a command on the Western frontier'. As the new commanding officer, Colonel Manderley wished to improve relations between the citizens and his soldiers. With that in mind, he, Winslow and the mayor of Shreveport—who would have been one of the victims in the plot—had come together and organized a 'Friendship Week'. During the seven days, there would be a variety of sporting, entertainment and social events, culminating with a Grand Ball on the Saturday.

'You wily old bas—gentleman—Uncle Alburgh,' Belle thought as she finished reading. 'With all that to look forward to, nobody will spare a thought for the speeches they heard. Nor about Selima's death. Not enough to query it deeply, anyway.'

Packing the money into his wallet, Sabot completed his change of clothing. Then he and Belle passed through the saloon's barroom towards its main entrance. Avoiding the various offers to stop and take a drink, by pointing out that the show was moving on early the following morning and so he and Selima wished to grab some sleep, he escorted the girl from the building.

There had been no sign of Mick in the barroom, but Belle soon detected him standing in the shadows across the street. Clearly he did not want his connection with the magician to be known. Instead of coming straight over, he waited until the couple had moved away from

the saloon before starting to cross the street. Belle
became aware of certain possibilities opened up by
Mick's actions. If he only would hold off from joining
them for a little while——

Obligingly, Mick did as Belle wished.

'Sabby!' the girl whispered, after they had covered
about a hundred yards along the practically empty
street. 'There's a man coming——.'

'So?'

'He's following us. He was lurking outside the saloon
and's been dogging our tracks ever since.'

'Why'd he do that, do you reckon?' Sabot inquired.

'It's our last night here. He'd know that you'd be
getting paid off and he's fixing to rob you.'

'It could be,' the magician admitted soberly, hiding
the amusement he felt. 'Shall I yell for the marshal?'

'That one-horse town knobhead!' Belle scoffed. 'He
couldn't catch a blown-off hat with three extra hands.
Anyway, I don't like turning anybody in to the john-
laws.'

'So what do we do?' Sabot challenged.

'Let's teach the bastard a lesson,' Belle suggested. 'I
think I know how we can do it.'

'All right,' the magician agreed, having heard the
girl's plan. 'We'll play it your way.'

Continuing to the end of the building they were
passing, Belle and Sabot turned into the alley. In the
shadows, they waited and listened to the sound of
Mick's feet drawing nearer. Whispering for Sabot to get
ready, the girl returned to the street. She timed her
arrival so that she walked straight into the burly man's
arms.

'What's the hurry, darlin'?' Mick demanded, dropping his hands to rest on Belle's hips, 'Did old——?'

'My, you're a big one,' Belle purred, not wanting a
premature exposure of Mick's connection with the
magician.

'If that's the way you like them, darlin',' Mick
grinned, feeling her body moving invitingly under his
palms. 'Then 'tis what I am.'

'I'll just bet you are,' Belle enthused, turning as if to walk away.

'Seeing's we're going the same way, darlin',' Mick commented, following and curling his right arm about her waist. 'Let's go together.'

Advancing a couple of steps side by side, Belle contrived to angle them so that their backs were to the mouth of the alley. Her right hand rose to rest on his, its thumb pressing against the rear-center of his knuckles. Curling her fingers under, she gently and provocatively tickled his palm as an aid in lulling him further into a sense of false security.

'Perhaps not all the way,' Belle drawled.

Tightening her grip on his hand, she stepped sideways with her right foot. Before he realized her intentions, she had hooked her left leg behind his right knee. Bending her knees slightly, to get below his center of gravity, she completed her escape. Working in smooth coordination, she propelled her left elbow rearwards against his solar plexus, kept her left leg rigid and thrust her body into his. Taken by surprise and off balance, Mick let out a startled curse. Belle released his hand, the arm flew from about her middle and he stumbled backwards into the alley. Unable to regain his equilibrium, he sat down hard.

'Stomp the bastard good, Sabby!' Belle hissed, spinning around. 'Teach him a lesson——!'

Instead of following the girl's excited advice, Sabot was laughing. So Belle reacted as she could be expected to have done if she had been genuine. Letting her words trail off, she displayed bewilderment at his lack of activity.

'Are you all right, Mick?' the magician inquired, moving forward.

'Wha——What——?' muttered the burly Irishman, shaking his head in a dazed and winded fashion. Then a dull, angry flush crept across his face and he started to lurch erect. 'Why you——!'

Watching Mick rise and look menacingly in her direction, Belle prepared to take measures for her protection. However, Sabot stepped between them. Flicking from inside his right sleeve, a shiny nickel-plated Remington Double Derringer settled its 'bird's head' butt in his waiting palm.

'Easy, Mick,' the magician ordered. 'She thought you was following to rob us and reckoned she could handle you. I see now that she could.'

Mumbling under his breath, Mick allowed his eyes to drop to the Remington. Although it dangled negligently at the magician's side, the Irishman was under no delusions as to its deadly qualities. Nor did he doubt that Sabot would use it if necessary.

'She near on bust my back!' Mick growled. 'I'll——'

'Do nothing,' Sabot finished for him.

'Just what the hell's going on?' Belle demanded, as she felt would be expected of her.

'It's all right, my dear,' Sabot replied, keeping his eyes on the other man and speaking over his shoulder. 'Mick's a friend of mine. We do business together. I should have told you, but I wanted to see how you'd make out.'

'Sure and it's slick the way you did it, darlin',' Mick went on, starting to grin. 'You wouldn't have Irish blood, would you?'

'You'd better come to the hotel with us, Mick,' Sabot suggested, giving Belle no chance to reply. 'We'll talk there.'

'That I'll do,' the Irishman agreed, looking at Belle. 'Can I take hold again without getting throwed over your head?'

'I wouldn't count on it,' Sabot warned and moved closer to whisper something in Mick's ear.

'If he's telling you I like girls, not fellers, he's right, Mick,' Belle said calmly. 'I'm not ashamed of it and your knowing will save us both time and inconvenience.'

'So that's the way of it?' Mick grunted, sounding disappointed. 'Well, 'tis everybody to their own tastes, I always say. Is she in it with us, Sabot?'

'I haven't asked,' the magician admitted. 'But I hope she will be.'

CHAPTER FOUR

U.S. Army Paymaster Robbed

Dressed in her 'harem girl' attire, Belle Boyd was seated in Sabot's dressing-room sharing a pot of coffee and doughnuts with the magician. They were waiting to start their first performance in Fort Worth, Texas, three weeks after their departure from Mooringsport.

Belle's time in Sabot's employment had not been wasted. Having been accepted at face value by her travelling companions, she had learned plenty about the Brotherhood For Southron Freedom. On first being told of its aims, she had displayed such enthusiasm that the magician had been convinced of her sincerity. So much so that he had not hesitated to speak freely with Mick in her presence.

According to the Irishman, with four exceptions, the Brotherhood had made good their escape from Shreveport. Brandt and his companion's fates were known; but nobody could discover what had happened to the two men who had followed Winslow from the theatre, and should have watched his house until the arrival of the 'arrest detail'. Sabot had guessed that they had taken alarm and fled when they realized the 'detail' was not coming; and Mick agreed that it was possible. Belle could have enlightened them on the matter, having dealt with the men in question, but felt disinclined to do so.

Continuing his report, Mick had said that de Richelieu—who appeared to be the supreme head of the Brotherhood—was taking the rifles and ammunition to

27

a ranch in Texas. As Sabot had apparently known the
ranch's location, Belle had not heard it mentioned. She
had not pressed the point, for to do so might have
aroused the magician's suspicion. Instead, she had
listened to the orders for their future activities. They
were to follow the original itinerary, but to act in a different manner than had been arranged. Instead of
spreading the news about the Shreveport incident, they
were merely to pass out pro-Secession propaganda and
select supporters for the movement.

In addition to improving her abilities as Sabot's
assistant, Belle had been required to help further the
Brotherhood's cause. The show had played one-night
stands at various towns since leaving Mooringsport. In
each, Sabot had given an informal dinner to carefully
selected members of the community. The selection had
been carried out by another member of the Brotherhood, whom Belle had not yet met. Traveling ahead of
the show, he decided who would be the most likely candidates and left a list of their names for Sabot to collect
at the towns' best hotels. After the third of the dinners,
at which she was required to act as hostess, Belle had
concluded that the unknown man was highly competent
in his duty.

At each dinner, the main topic of conversation had
been the evils of living under Yankee domination. Belle
had identified the guests as malcontents, trouble-causers
and rabid Secessionists of the kind she had always
mistrusted as much as violently pro-Unionists. Fanatics
of any kind had always been dangerous.

Once the magician had felt sure of his audience, he
had told them of the forces at work to 'liberate' the suffering Southern States. When that happened, he had
gone on, there would be positions of power, influence,
importance—and wealth—in store for the men who had
played an active part during the early days of the
struggle. Men like themselves, in fact, if they had the
courage, and sufficient loyalty to the Confederate
cause, to lend a hand in the work that lay ahead. The
arguments being presented had been calculated to ap-

peal to the guests' patriotism, personal ego, avarice and other basic human emotions. Always the message had been there.

Give money to purchase arms!

Make ready for the day of reckoning with the Yankees!

THE SOUTH WILL RISE AGAIN!

There had been oaths of allegiance and secrecy sworn at the dinners. Arrangements had been discussed for the collection of the donations contributed, or gathered from others, by the guests and turned over to the Brotherhood's funds.

Always when that point had been reached, the listeners had grown cagey and unresponsive. While willing to support another attempt at Secession, and to donate—or at least collect—the money, none of them had been willing to hand it over without some convincing proof that the Brotherhood's intentions were honorable. Waving aside as unimportant, or as evidence of his guests' sound business sense, the comments about not doubting his word, Sabot had promised that a sign would be forthcoming in the near future. He had never offered to name a date, but had insisted that no donations would be accepted until the proof had been forthcoming. That had always impressed the listeners. It had also produced replies that he, or some other member of the Brotherhood, could contact their supporters *after* the promised sign had become a proven and established fact.

To help her play her part the more successfully, Sabot had purchased Belle a more presentable wardrobe. He had insisted that she tone down her facial makeup and generally improve her appearance. Dressed in stylish clothes and displaying a gracious yet somewhat condescending manner which had been highly impressive—especially in the small towns where such sophistication was rarely seen—it had been her duty to pave the way for the real purpose of the dinners. Her shame-faced admissions of how she had been driven onto the stage —breaking her dear mama's heart in the process—

through Yankee oppression had invariably won her much sympathy and guided the conversation along the required lines.

Belle had had some heart-searchings before she had decided to play her part so well. After serious consideration, she had concluded that the end justified the means. By presenting an image of complete loyalty and proving herself to be a capable ally, she would be all the more likely to be taken into the confidence of the Brotherhood's leaders.

The trend of the meetings had confirmed that her decision was a reasonably safe one. Until the promised sign was given, there was little danger of the guests carrying out their duties. Once it happened, if the need to take action arose, Belle knew the men in each town. They could be arrested before they did any harm.

Despite her growing knowledge of the Brotherhood, Belle had not yet managed to learn the identity of 'the Frenchman'. Although she had never heard of him mentioned in such a manner, de Richelieu had seemed the most likely candidate by virtue of his name. She had decided to leave positive identification until a more convenient date. There were other matters, of greater importance than personal vengeance, to occupy her.

Belle had heard enough to know that the Brotherhood was a large and growing organization. From what Sabot, Mick—who acted as liaison between the magician and the mysterious selector—and the other men in the show had told her, de Richelieu had assembled a fighting force. Men, wanted by the law in their own States, or willing to fight if necessary, had been dispatched to the ranch. So far, she had been unable to discover its location. In fact, she had reached the conclusion that none of her companions were better informed as to its whereabouts. Avoiding displaying undue, possible suspicious, interest, she remained alert for any hint concerning it. She was also on watch constantly for the promised sign.

Belle's arrival at Fort Worth had, in one rspect, strengthened her chances of survival.

Having won Sabot's trust, the girl had learned the names of the towns where they would be performing. Her reason had been, she had claimed, to warn him of any in which the law might take an unwanted interest in her arrival. Wanting to avoid such an eventuality, the magician had supplied the required details. Later, before leaving Mooringsport, she had contrived to send a telegraph message secretly to Winslow and requested that he should forward her property to Fort Worth.

That afternoon, Belle had visited the Overland Stage Line's depot and was told that her trunk had arrived. Without revealing her true identity, she had persuaded the agent to let her open it in the privacy of a rear room. Taking out her Hessian boots, black riding breeches, dark-blue shirt, Western-style gunbelt and ivory-handled Dance Bros. Navy revolver, she had locked the trunk again. Then she had arranged for it, and a written report of her activities, to be shipped to the wife of the Secret Service's Texan-based coordinator. Mrs. Edge would know what to do with Belle's property.

Since Belle was satisfied that Sabot and his men trusted her, she did not worry about the clothing being found in her possession. They accepted her pretense of being a lesbian and she felt sure that she could explain away the garments, gunbelt and Dance. However, she had not taken chances of being seen with them. Selecting a time when she had known that the others would be at the theatre, she had taken her property to the hotel. Concealing it under the other garments in the trunk which Sabot had purchased for her to use, she had locked it and joined the men.

Belle was comforted by the knowledge that she had the clothing and revolver in case of strenuous activity or the need to escape.

The door of the dressing-room flew open. Waving a copy of the *Fort Worth Globe*, the baritone entered followed by the two comedians. All of them showed considerable excitement.

'Is this it, Sabot?' demanded the singer, holding the

newspaper so that Belle and the magician could see its front page.

The headlines, large—and seeming larger, sprang out to attract Belle's attention. A cold, anxious sensation bit at her.

U.S. PAYMASTER ROBBED!
$10,000.00 HAUL FOR GANG.

Was the robbery the promised incident that might trigger off and embroil the Unionist and Confederate States in another war?

'Let me see it,' Sabot commanded, sounding genuinely surprised and hopeful.

With an effort, Belle concealed her impatience. She waited until Sabot had read the story, then asked if she could take a look. Grinning, he handed it over.

'Is it?' the singer, Stapler by name, repeated.

'I don't know,' Sabot admitted. 'Mick hasn't said that anything was planned, and there isn't anything in the instructions.'

While the men talked, Belle began to read. Nothing in the story intimated that the incident had been organized for propaganda, or financial gain, by the Brotherhood.

In the first place, the robbery had taken place over two weeks earlier. It seemed unlikely that the organization would have kept quiet about their participation if they had been involved.

Secondly, the descriptions of the three men who had committed the crime struck the girl as being vaguely familiar.

Apparently the trio had learned that the Paymaster would be transporting the money from a Sergeant Magoon of the 8th Cavalry. With his connivance, they had planned the robbery. He had then been shot by them, along with the Paymaster and the rest of the small escort. News of the theft had not been released sooner to increase the chances of apprehending the culprits. A reward of ten thousand dollars was offered for the arrest of each of the trio. According to the newspaper, the Texas Rangers and Colonel Edge, of the Army's Adjutant General's Department, held high hopes of making an early arrest.*

No mention of the Cause. Not the slightest suggestion that the robbery had been perpetrated to help the Confederate States regain their liberty. Yet there was something in the story which perturbed the girl. Just what, she found herself unable to decide.

Certainly it was not the fact that the Adjutant General's Department was involved which aroused her interest. In addition to his military duties, Colonel Edge acted as coordinator for the Secret Service in Texas. Both his capacities would lead him to be deeply concerned by the robbery. Probably it had been by his orders that news of it was supressed for so long.

Another, small, headline on the front page caught Belle's attention as she stood turning the matter over in her mind.

GOVERNOR ACTS TO STOP RANGE WAR.

If Belle had not glimpsed one of the names in that item, she might have dismissed it as unimportant to her assignment. On the face of it, there was no possible connection between the robbery and the second story. Nor, unless there was much more to it, could the Governor of Texas' intervention be regarded as forming a part of the Brotherhood's promised sign.

Ranchers Shangai Pierce, Miffin Kennedy and Richard King were protesting about a beef contract which had been awarded by the U.S. Army to General Ole Devil Hardin's OD Connected ranch. All the men concerned, particularly the latter, had been loyal to the South in the War. So de Richelieu would not be able to make propaganda profit from the selection.

According to the stories, tempers were high amongst the ranchers. To prevent a range war erupting, Gover-

* The full newspaper story is given in: HELL IN THE PALO DURO.

nor Stanton Howard had asked the protesting trio and the OD Connected's segundo—since his injury while riding a bad horse had left him crippled,* General Hardin was unavailable—to join him at the end of the month in San Antonio de Bexar. It was hoped that an amicable solution could be reached at the gathering. The first shipment of cattle—which were going by sea from Brownsville to New Orleans—would be dispatched as arranged, under the care of several well-known members of the OD Connected's work force.

Frowning in concentration and oblivious of the men's conversation, Belle returned her gaze to the coverage of the robbery. She read the descriptions of the Caxton brothers, Edward Jason and Matthew 'Boy', and of their companion-in-crime, Alvin 'Comanche' Blood, noting the tribe of Indians mentioned and paying especial care to scrutinize the weapons they were alleged to carry. From there, her eyes took in once more the name of the disloyal, betrayed and murdered non-commissioned officer.

'Poor Sergeant Magoon,' Belle mused, thoughts racing through her head and a theory forming. 'He had so many friends at the OD Connected. If Dusty wasn't going to attend this peace conference, and Mark or Lon weren't on their way to New Orleans with the cattle, I just bet they'd all be out hunting down his killers.'

'What do you make of it, Selima?' asked Hugh Downend, the straight man of the cross-talk duo, cutting in on the girl's theorizing and bringing her back to reality with a jolt.

'Of what?' Belle asked, hardly able to remember anything of the conversation that she had only half heard between the men.

'You looked like you're giving this affair some thought,' Miller Dunco, the comic of the pair, told her.

'I was,' the girl admitted. 'Boy! What I'd give to meet those Caxton brothers and ''Comanche'' Blood. Anybody who'd do that to the Yankees is all right from

* Told in the 'The Paint' episode of: *THE FASTEST GUN IN TEXAS*.

where I sit—Hey though! Are they in the Brotherhood?'

Belle felt that she had covered her obvious preoc-
cupation in an adequate manner. Certainly the men appeared to be satisfied with her explanation. While her
final words had raised a point in which the men were interested, the baritone eyed her in a speculative manner.

'Do you know them?' Stapler asked.

Ever since the singer had taken her knee in the groin,
he had been faintly but definitely hostile. He was a com-
pulsive womanizer, who tried to make a conquest in
every town they visited. While he was frequently successful, his failure with the slender, beautiful girl had
rankled. Her presence with the show had been a con-
stant reminder of the incident; nor had the other men
allowed him to forget that there was one girl who would
not respond to his charms. In view of Sabot's orders,
Stapler had kept his distance; but he had always made it
clear that he disliked 'Selima'.

'Why should I know them, *Mr.* Stapler?' Belle
countered, laying emphasis on the honorific in a way
which expressed a mutual dislike.

'I thought you're the biggest lady bandit since Belle
Starr,' Stapler answered, referring to her frequent hints
concerning her 'criminal activities'.

'I've heard it said that *you're* God's own gift to
womanhood,' Belle countered viciously. 'But that
doesn't mean you've laid every woman West of the Big
Muddy. Some of them have better ta——'

'Let it ride, both of you!' Sabot snapped, being
desirous of averting an open clash with its danger of one
or the other performer quitting his show.

'These mixed marriages never work out,' Dunco went
on, rolling his eyes at his partner and winking.

'I'm with Dick, though,' Downend remarked. 'Not
about you, Selima. But how do we answer if we're asked
at the dinner?'

'Say "yes",' Dunco suggested, his smooth, fat face
aglow with excitement.

'I don't agree,' Belle put in, aware of what might happen if they followed the comic's advice and were

believed. 'If we say "yes" and it comes out that they weren't doing it for the Brotherhood, we'll be discredited and mistrusted. Everybody will think we're just trying to slicker them out of their money.'

'That's true enough,' Sabot conceded. 'Look, Mick's due here any day with our pay from de Richelieu——'

'Pay?' Belle put in.

'Just a little added inducement for us to continue with the good work,' Dunco smirked. 'Didn't Sabby mention it?'

'I wanted it as a surprise for you,' the magician apologized and, seeing that Belle did not look impressed with the explanation, changed the subject. 'If de Richelieu has seen this story and they're not part of the Brotherhood, he'll have sent us orders on how to act. So we'll wait until Mick arrives before we decide what to say.'

'About this pay, Sabby?' Belle queried, figuring that a real 'Melanie Beauchampaine' would do so.

'It's a bonus for our work,' the magician elaborated. 'I wasn't trying to cheat you, Selima.'

'Why not, I'd do it to you,' Belle smiled. 'Whooee! This brotherhood's bigger and richer than I imagined.'

'They've got some powerful foreign backing, from what we've been told,' Dunco commented.

Belle had already heard, during Sabot's interrupted Shreveport show, that the Brotherhood was being sponsored by an undisclosed European country. That was one of the details she must check out, discovering if she could which nation was involved.

'Come on, fellers,' Sabot said, preventing Belle from probing deeper into the subject. 'We're on soon.'

The meeting broke up on that note.

Mick arrived the next evening. Meeting with Sabot and the other performers in the magician's dressing-room, he confirmed that the Brotherhood had not been involved in the robbery. Belle's stock as a shrewd judge of a situation was enhanced by his next piece of information. De Richelieu had sent word for them to disclaim all responsibility and had given an identical reason to the girls for having reached the decision.

'On top of which,' Mick went on, 'he says he doesn't want folks thinking we're a bunch of thieves, murderers and such like.'

'Very wise,' Sabot confirmed, hoping that the Irishman would remember to mention his support to their leader. 'It might scare off the more respectable candidates.'

'You've been to the ranch, huh, Mick?' Belle remarked casually, in the pause which followed Sabot's words, acting as if she was making casual conversation.

'I sure have,' the Irishman enthused, showing that his first visit had left a deep impression. 'There's well over a hundred men there already, trained, armed with Henry repeaters and r'aring to lay into the Yankees.'

'Good for them!' Belle whooped, sounding genuinely delighted. 'I can't wait to meet them.'

' 'Tis likely you will, darling',' Mick assured her.

'Come on, Selima,' Sabot put in amiably, eyeing her street clothes. 'Nobody will believe I rescued you from "a life of sin in the Sultan of Tripoli's harem" if you go on dressed like this.'

Accepting the obvious dismissal, Belle left the room. She hoped that she might be able to pump Mick for further information after the performance. However, he had departed before she was free to do so.

That night, in the privacy of her hotel room, Belle wrote a report for Colonel Edge. In it, she gave the latest information and mentioned how serious she believed the situation to be. An armed force of over a hundred desperate, ruthless men would be a formidable weapon in the Brotherhood's hands. So she warned that she would require assistance to deal with the menace. To show that she had noticed a possible connection between the stories in the *Fort Worth Globe*, she concluded her request for reinforcements by saying:

'Send me three regiments of cavalry—or Dusty Fog.'

CHAPTER FIVE

My Name Is Belle Boyd

'Selima, darling,' Dunco said, walking into Belle's room without knocking, as she was packing to leave Fort Worth. 'Can you lend me——?'

The words trailed off as he stared at the riding boots and black breeches which lay on the bed. Having intended to hide them more thoroughly amongst her conventional clothing, the girl had unpacked them. She had forgotten to lock her door and was caught out.

'I bought them and these with my bonus,' Belle explained, thinking fast and producing the gunbelt with the Dance in its holster.

An understanding expression flickered onto Dunco's face. Being a homosexual who enjoyed wearing women's clothing, he appreciated the reason for 'Selima' making such unusual purchases. Many of the bull-dykes* he had met donned male attire to emphasize their 'masculinity'.

'Very fashionable, I'm sure,' Dunco simpered. 'Can you loan me a needle and some thread, dear, I've a button to sew on and I can't find mine.'

Belle obligingly produced the required items. Watching the man leave, she gave a wry smile. Forgetting to turn the key had been a dangerous oversight which she would have to avoid in the future. However, no real harm—in fact, possibly some good—had been done. She did not doubt that Dunco would tell the other

* Bull-dyke: dominant, 'masculine' partner in a lesbian relationship.

members of the show of what he had seen. In which case, having accepted her sexual aberration, they would regard the purchase in the same manner as Dunco. So it no longer mattered if they should see the garments and weapon. The fact that the Dance was a cap-and-ball revolver from a defunct Confederate firearm's manufacturing company would aid the deception. It would be regarded as nothing more than an added prop in her pretense of being a man.

At the dinner the previous evening, the usual discussion had run its almost predictable course. When the subject of the robbery had been introduced, Belle had seen that de Richelieu's conclusions were correct. At least three of the guests, respectable businessmen with real or imagined grudges against the Federal Congress, had shown relief on being told that the Brotherhood would not stoop to robbery and murder —even of Yankee soldiers—to achieve their aims.

Moving on to Dallas, the show played a week there. No more reports of the robbery appeared in the newspapers and the proposed peace conference was also forgotten. Nothing out of the ordinary happened until the last night. Then Stapler's dislike for Belle took a more active form. It had come about because she had accidentally knocked over a piece of scenery, which had fallen with a clatter and ruined the finale of his act. In the wings, he had accused Belle of doing it deliberately and a heated scene was averted only by Sabot's intervention.

The dinner was to be held in the banqueting room of the Cattlemen's Hotel. As had become the usual procedure, Belle and Sabot had arrived before the others to supervise the seating arrangements. They were alone in the room when the doors were thrust open and Stapler entered. Hanging onto his arm was a buxom, good-looking redhead. From the cut of her clothes and general appearance, the baritone's companion did not come into the socially-acceptable 'good woman' class. On top of that, both she and her escort looked to have taken just a little too much to drink. Shoving the doors together behind them, the couple made their way towards Belle. They halted, arm in arm, before the girl and were obviously looking for trouble.

'My, my, look at our little Selima,' Stapler mocked, running his eyes up and down Belle's elegant ball gown in derision. 'She looks almost like a woman, don't she, Bertha?'

'You're drunk!' Sabot growled, turning from the table at which he was standing.

'I've had a few, but not enough to make me like her,' growled the baritone. 'What do you make of her, Bertha?'

'Dykes of any kind turn my guts,' the redhead answered. 'And bull——'

'Hold your voices down, blast you!' the magician hissed, walking forward. 'And, if this's the best you can do, you'd better stay away from the dinner.'

'What's up, Sabby?' Stapler demanded. 'Ain't Bertha good enough to meet your friends. If a dirty little dy——'

Gliding forward a pace, Belle caused the baritone to chop off his words abruptly. She was responding as 'Melanie Beauchampaine' would have done. However, her dislike for the singer—and a subconscious detestation of being regarded as a lesbian, no matter how much the untrue supposition assisted her work—helped to bring the reaction.

Belle's right hand lashed towards the singer's face. Not as a slap, but in a well-aimed, skilfully delivered punch. Pivoting from the waist, she put her full weight behind the swing of the blow. Her knuckles arrived against the edge of his jaw hard enough to snap his head sideways and send him staggering.

Taken by surprise at the speed and force of Belle's response, Stapler did not find time to release Bertha's arm before he was hit. So he dragged the redhead with him as he made his involuntary retreat. Snatching her arm free, Bertha let out a furious screech. Then she hurled herself towards the slender girl with crooked, long-nailed fingers reaching out to take hold.

Spitting blood and mumbling obscenities, Stapler caught his balance with an effort. He retained his footing and made as if to follow Bertha. Darting forward, sallow features contorted by rage, Sabot intervened. Catching the singer by the shoulder, the magician jerked him around and followed Belle's original means of dealing with him. Caught between the thighs by Sabot's knee, the baritone gave vent to a croaking, tormented moan. If the anguish on his face, as he doubled over, was anything to go by, Stapler would not be much of a bed-mate for Bertha that night.

Nor, in view of what was happening, would the buxom redhead be harboring many romantic notions.

Having expected a similar response from Bertha, Belle was prepared to meet it. However, she had no intention of becoming involved in a prolonged hair-tearing brawl if she could avoid it. So she figured out a way which would settle their differences quickly and with a reasonable chance of permanency.

Snatching up the hem of her gown to leave her legs unencumbered, Belle allowed Bertha's claw-like hands almost to reach her head. Then she side-stepped to the left, twisting and inclining her body at the hips in the same direction. Missing her target, but unable to halt her forward momentum, Bertha continued to advance. Like a flash, Belle turned her body, standing on her left leg, and swung her right knee as hard as she could into the redhead's belly.

Bertha's whalebone corsets were no protection against such an attack. In fact, their construction tended to magnify its effect. Feeling as if her stomach was being thrust back into her spine, she let out an agonizing croak. With hands clutching at the point of impact, she doubled over and stumbled on a couple of paces.

Spinning around, Belle grabbed hold of the redhead's bustle in both hands. With a sudden, jerking upwards heave, she snatched Bertha's feet from the floor. The woman turned a somersault and landed with a crash on her back.

Knowing that 'Melanie Beauchampaine' would not be likely to let her assailant off so lightly, Belle acted in the manner of her assumed identity. Turning, she moved around and stood astride the winded, helpless woman's body. Sinking to her knees and straddling Bertha's ample bosom, Belle settled her weight on it. Grabbing a healthy double handful of the red hair, the girl raised and thumped the woman's head on the floor.

The doors were thrown open and, followed by a couple of waiters, the other members of the show flooded in. Glancing at them, Sabot indicated Stapler as he crouched, moaning and retching on his knees.

'Get that bastard out of here,' the magician ordered. 'And pull Selima off of that tail-peddler* before she caves her skull in.'

Hurrying across the room, the cross-talk duo grabbed Belle by the armpits and lifted her erect. Although she made a token resistance, she was pleased that there had been such a prompt intervention. Bertha was lying limp and unconscious, so the girl had wanted an excuse to end her attack. However, she must play her part out thoroughly.

"Lemme go!' Belle demanded, struggling in the two men's grasp. 'Lemme get at her——'

'That wouldn't be fair,' Dunco pointed out. 'Not unless we brought her round first. She's out colder than last week's pot roast.'

'But not near on so attractive to look at,' Belle admitted, grinning and ceasing her 'attempts' at regaining her freedom. Then she frowned and snapped. 'Where's that no-good, screeching, off-key lantern†?'

'He's not feeling too good,' Dunco grinned as he and his companion released the girl's arms. 'In fact, I bet he feels more like a gelatine‡ than a baritone right now.'

Turning, Belle saw that two of the musicians were hoisting Stapler to his feet. Beyond them, Sabot was

---

* Tail-peddler: a prostitute of the cheapest variety.
† Lantern: derogatory name for an inferior baritone.
‡ Gelatine: a tenor with a high, tremolo tone.

apologizing to the hotel's employees for the disturbance.

'He's had too much to drink, gentlemen,' the magician announced. 'I assure you that there won't be a repetition of his disgraceful behavior.'

'He sure looks like he's learned his lesson,' the senior of the waiters drawled, studying the baritone's agonized expression and general symptoms of suffering. 'You want for us to give him the old heave-ho?'

'We'll attend to him, and her,' Sabot promised and, continuing his platitudes, he edged the men from the room. Closing the door behind them, he swung towards Stapler. 'You stupid, no-good, drunken son-of-a-bitch!'

'Y-y-y-f—bast—!' the baritone moaned.

Advancing, Sabot lashed the back of his right hand across the man's face. Then he grabbed hold of Stapler's lapels and wrenched him bodily from the musicians' grasp. With a surging heave, the magician propelled the baritone across the room to collide with the wall back first. Looking even more demoniac because he had followed his usual habit of retaining his stage make-up and clothing, Sabot rushed after the man.

Nauseated, suffering agonies, and with his mind befuddled by Sabot's rough handling, Stapler could still think well enough to realize his danger. He had seen enough examples of Sabot's evil side to believe that his good looks—perhaps his very life—might be in jeopardy.

'N—No!' Stapler croaked, throwing up his hands to shield his face from the expected attack.

Sabot made a disgusted sound deep in his throat, surveying the cowering singer with deep contempt. Then he took hold of the other's wrists and wrenched them away, glaring into the sweat-soddened, pain-filled and frightened face.

'You no-account, useless, womanizing bastard!' the magician snarled. 'I ought to cripple you so's you'd lose this craving to lay every she-male you set eyes on.

Or alter your face so thay won't look twice your way, except to retch——.'

'D—Don't!' the baritone moaned.

'I won't, this time,' Sabot promised, stepping away. 'But only because you're useful in the show. The next time you make a fool play like this, I'll make you wish you'd never been born.' Having delivered the warning, he turned to the other men and continued, 'See that he gets back to the hotel. And take that tail-peddling whore away from here. Make sure she doesn't come back.'

'Sure, Sabby,' replied the orchestra's leader. 'Do you reckon he'll be—all right—left alone, after what's happened?'

'If you mean, do I think he'll run out on us, or lay information with the town clowns, the answer's "no",' the magician stated confidently. 'They couldn't prove anything against us, without catching us in the act. And, anyways, I know about a girl in Vicksburg whose folks'd just love to hear where he's at.'

'Y—You wouldn't tell them?' Stapler gasped, showing that he understood the full implications behind the comment. 'If they laid hands on me——.'

'That's what I mean,' Sabot purred. 'You're safer working with me—as long as *I* want it that way!'

'S—sure, Sabby!' the singer whined. 'I—I wouldn't cross you——.'

'It's nice to know *that*,' Sabot sneered. 'Get going.'

After the singer and the unconscious woman had been removed, the dinner went by uneventfully.

Meeting Belle and Sabot at breakfast the following morning, Stapler made no reference to the events of the previous evening. If Bertha harbored any ill-feelings towards the girl who had mishandled her so effectively, which she probably did, she had sufficient prudence not to come and make them known. In fact, Belle never saw her again.

Coming out of the post office later that afternoon, having mailed her latest report to Colonel Edge, Belle noticed Stapler was across the street. However, the singer did not look in her direction and strolled into a

saloon without displaying any awareness of her presence. She concluded that he had not seen her and carried
on with her intention of going to the theatre.

In addition to developing her competence as Sabot's
assistant, Belle had taken a genuine interest in his work.
Soon after their first meeting in Mooringsport, flattered
by her obvious appreciation and admiration for his
talents, he had started to teach her how to do some of
his illusions. Always a quick learner, and being an ex-
ceptionally intelligent, nimble-fingered girl, she had
made rapid progress in acquiring the basic sleight-of-
hand moves that formed the essence of a stage
magician's act. It had been far easier for her to gain
proficiency in the more spectacular mechanical illusions
with which Sabot climaxed his performance. Taking an
active part in them, and helping to set them up, had
made her wise to how they were carried out. By the time
the show had reached Dallas, the rest of the performers
had begun to warn Sabot jokingly that 'Selima' was
likely to take over the act.

Leaving Dallas, the party traveled on the Overland
stagecoaches as they continued with the tour. Still the
mysterious selector roamed ahead of them, leaving
letters of guidance for Sabot in every town they visited.

Waxahachie, Martin, Cameron and Temple fell
behind them as one-night stands. Although each was its
respective county's seat, none had been of sufficient
size to sustain the show for a longer stay. The party were
moving roughly southwest, in the direction of Austin.

With a week to go before the end of the month, Belle
still had not received replies to her reports. Having mail
addressed to her, even in her assumed name, would have
been more dangerous than dispatching an occasional
letter, so she had not been expecting any. She was
looking forward to playing at the state's capital. Once
there, she would be able to arrange a meeting with
Colonel Edge and exchange verbal information.
Perhaps too her request for assistance would be given its
answer by Dusty Fog being in the city.

Before her arrival, she hoped to learn the location of de Richelieu's ranch.

While Belle found herself in a position to acquire the desired information, concerning the ranch, the chance to hand it over was not presented to her.

On reading his instructions at Temple, in Bell County, Sabot had informed the others that their visit to Austin had been canceled. Instead, they would make their way to San Antonio de Bexar. They had moved on to play one night in Blanco County's Johnson City. From there, they had traveled farther southwest to what they had assumed would be the scene of their next engagement.

Climbing out of the stagecoach at sundown, the entertainers looked with considerable disfavor at the straggling main—almost only—street of Los Cabestrillo. The usual variety of business, social and professional buildings were scattered haphazardly along its length. They were a mixture of heat-baked adobe and sun-warped planks, pointing to a fusion of Mexican and Anglo-Saxon architecture that was functional if not artistic or aesthetically pleasing to the eye.

'Lordy lord!' Belle groaned. 'If anybody gave me a necklace like this, I'd ram it down their throats.'

'How's that?' Dunco inquired.

'*Cabestrillo*,' Belle elaborated. 'It's Spanish for "necklace". Only I wouldn't use that in your act. The citizens might not like it.'

'This's a hell of a looking town,' Stapler complained. 'It's the worst since Mooringsport.'

'Why worry?' grinned Downend. 'We'll get paid whether we play to a handful of rubes or a full theatre.'

'Isn't that Mick across the street?' Belle inquired, pointing to the front of the imposing—a full *two* stories high—Longhorn Hotel.

''Yes,' Sabot agreed, looking puzzled. 'I wonder what he wants?'

'Here he comes,' Dunco commented needlessly.

Dressed like a cowhand, with an Army Colt holstered

at his right thigh, the Irishman slouched over. He offered to help tote the party's baggage, acting as if they
were strangers. Then, after the coach had moved off
and the agent's crew had dispersed, he looked around to
make sure that they were not likely to be overheard.

'I've got a wagon at the livery barn,' Mick announced.

'What for?' Sabot demanded.

'To take you out to the ranch,' Mick explained and
was pleased by the reaction to his words. 'There's
something big coming off and Colonel de Richelieu
wants you to know about it. Besides, he doesn't want
you doing the show and giving the dinner here. Folks in
town don't know what's going on at the ranch and he
doesn't want anybody starting to think things.'

'That's reasonable,' Sabot admitted. 'Let's get the
gear down to the wagon and ready to move.'

'Aw, Sabby,' Belle protested. 'I'm hungry. Can't we
eat before we leave?'

'It might be as well,' Mick agreed. 'We've a fair ride
ahead of us.'

'All right,' the magician confirmed, much to Belle's
delight. 'We'll load up, grab a meal, then go.'

While working, Belle felt a surge of excitement. At
last she had some definite information. The ranch was
within fairly easy distance of Los Cabestrillo. Close
enough to make the town a useful point from which to
start a search. Most likely the local marshal could be of
help in deciding which property was being used by the
Brotherhood.

One thing was for sure. No matter how great the risk,
Belle must pass on the news to Colonel Edge. Then, if
she should be recognized or suspected, the Secret Service would have been warned.

The question was, how could she send her message?

Mick's comments about the people of the town
supplied Belle with a possible answer. Telegraph wires
glinted in the last, dying rays of the sun, stretching from
the Overland Stage Depot out across the range. There

was her means of communication, if only she could reach it without arousing suspicion.

'Phew!' the girl ejaculated, looking with distaste at the wagon. 'Riding in that will play hell with my good clothes.'

'Change into your old things,' Mick suggested.

'I don't have them any more,' Belle pointed out. 'I burned them as soon as I got something decent.'

'You could always put your riding breeches on,' Dunco remarked, just as Belle had hoped somebody would.

'Hey!' she grinned. 'That's an idea. I'll do it.'

'Not until after we've fed,' Sabot protested. 'You can do it while us fellers sink a couple of drinks.'

Belle concealed her elation, knowing that the magician had once more played into her hands.

After a decent meal at the hotel, Belle returned to the livery barn. It was deserted, which was just how she wanted it to be. Working swiftly, she boarded the wagon and unlocked her trunk. Changing into her masculine attire and buckling on her gunbelt, she decided against placing percussion caps on the Dance's nipples. To do so would consume valuable seconds; and she did not expect to need the weapon. So she placed it in her holster, packed away her discarded clothing and walked from the building. Her appearance would help to convince the telegraph operator of her *bona fides* when she made her request for assistance.

Although Belle kept alert as she made her way to the Overland Stage Depot, she saw nothing to alarm her. Reaching the building, she found it deserted except for an elderly man who was about to go out through the side door. He wore the dress of a clerk and sported a green eye-shield, implying that he was of a higher grade than a mere hostler.

'Excuse me, sir,' Belle said, hurrying around the corner and meeting the man in the alley. 'Are you the telgraphist?'

'I am, young lady,' the man admitted, after giving her

a long, appraising scrutiny. 'Can I do anything for you?'

'Yes. My name is Belle Boyd——'

Just an instant too late Belle realized that the man was staring too intently at something beyond her.

Or *somebody*!

'So you're *Belle Boyd*!' said Stapler's voice from behind the girl and it throbed with gloating triumph.

Spinning around, Belle twisted her righthand palm outwards to the ivory butt of the Dance. While the revolver was empty, she could use it to bluff the baritone; or pistol-whip him.

Neither chance was permitted!

To her horror, Belle completed her turn to find herself face to face with Stapler *and* Dunco. The comic looked bewildered, but the baritone clearly had no doubts about what action he should take.

Gliding in fast, Stapler sank his right fist savagely into Belle's stomach. Winded and gagging for breath, she still had the wits to try to draw away as she folded over. The attempt was only partially successful. Instead of taking her in the center of the face, Stapler's rising left knuckles met her forehead and lifted her erect. With everything spinning crazily around before her eyes, Belle was helpless and defenseless. Across hurled the bariton's right hand, smashing against her jaw. Flung sideways, her limp body measured its length on the ground. She did not feel the impact.

CHAPTER SIX

Isn't That Captain Fog?

'Captain *Fog*!' ejaculated the desk clerk at the
Longhorn Hotel in Los Cabestrillo, jerking his gaze
from the register to study the man who had just inscribed the name he read out with such interest. 'Are
you Captain Dusty Fog, sir?'

There was frank and open admiration in the clerk's
voice and manner, for the newly arrived guest bore a
name that was honored, respected and revered
throughout the length and breadth of Texas.

At a mere seventeen years of age, Dustine Edward
Marsden Fog had been promoted in the field to captain
and given command of the Texas Light Cavalry's hard-
riding, harder-fighting Company 'C'. From then until
the end of the War, he had built up a reputation as a
military raider equaling that of Dixie's other maestros,
Turner Ashby and the 'Gray Ghost', John Singleton
Mosby. Ranging over the less-publicized Arkansas
battlefront, he had matched their efforts in making life
unbearable for the Yankees.* Rumor claimed that he
had supported Belle Boyd, the Rebel Spy, on two of her
missions. Less public knowledge was that he had also
prevented two pro-Unionist fanatics from stirring up
the Texas' Indian tribes into a rampage that would have
decimated much of the Lone Star State.† Also to his
credit had been his capture and eventual destruction of a

* Told in: *UNDER THE STARS AND BARS* and *KILL DUSTY
FOG!*
† Told in: *THE DEVIL GUN.*

51

great cannon with which the Union's Army of Arkansas had hoped to swing the balance of power into their favor.*

With the War over and his uncle crippled and confined to a wheelchair, Dusty had taken on the responsibility of being segundo of the great OD Connected ranch. He had gained the name as cowhand, trail driver and trail boss par excellence,† as well as being a town-taming peace officer of considerable ability.‡

Never slow to give credit to their favorite sons' good qualities, Texans also claimed that Dusty Fog was the fastest, most accurate and efficient handler of two Colts ever to draw breath; also that there were few men who could come close to matching his skill in a bare-handed brawl.

From where he was standing, the desk clerk admitted mentally that Captain Dusty Fog looked just as he had always imagined.

Six foot three in height, with a tremendous spread of shoulders and tapering to a lean waist and long, powerful legs, the man had curly, golden blond hair and a strong, tanned, almost classically handsome face. Encircled by a black leather band, sporting decorative silver conchas, a white J.B. Stetson hat of Texas style sat jauntily on the back of his head. Its fancy, thin-plaited leather *barbiquejo* chin strap dangled loosely under his jaw. Around his throat, a scarlet silk bandana trailed long ends over a tan-colored shirt that had obviously been tailored to fit his giant-muscled frame. His Levi trousers were of an equally excellent fit, their cuffs were turned back and hanging outside high-heeled, spur-bearing, fancy stitched boots.

While the clerk studied the big blond's clothing, his main attention was on the other's armament.

* Told in: *THE BIG GUN.*
 † Told in: *GOODNIGHT'S DREAM, FROM HIDE AND HORN* and *TRAIL BOSS.*
 ‡ Told in: *QUIET TOWN, THE TROUBLE BUSTERS, THE MAKING OF A LAWMAN, THE TOWN TAMERS* and *THE SMALL TEXAN.*

Around the blond's waist was cinched a brown, hand-carved *buscadero* gunbelt made by a master craftsman. In its contoured, carefully-designed holsters—the bottoms of which were secured to his thighs by pigging thongs—rode a brace of ivory-handled Colt Cavalry Peacemakers. Their metal work showed the deep rich blue of the manufacturer's Best Citizens' Finish, but they were functional and effective fighting weapons for all of that.

'That's what the book says,' the blond giant answered, his voice deep, amiable and that of a well-educated Texan. 'Room Twenty-One, huh?'

'Yes, sir,' the clerk confirmed and indicated a boy who was hovering nearby, taking everything in with eager eyes and ears. 'I'll have the bellhop help you with your things, Captain Fog.'

'Shucks, I'll tote my own gear,' the blond countered, holding the heavy low-horned, double-girthed* range saddle—which had a Winchester rifle in its boot, a long rope coiled at its horn and a bulky bed roll lashed to its cantle—without apparent effort. 'Maybe you'll fetch along the key, *amigo*?'

'Yes, sir, Cap'n Fog!' the youngster replied, displaying an unusual zeal in the performance of his duties. Taking the key, he escorted the giant to the stairs. As they started to ascend, he indicated the gunbelt and went on, 'Is them the new-fangled Colts you used when you floating-outfit fellers whipped the whole blasted Mexican Army last year?'

Emerging from the barroom, on the left of the entrance lobby, two men stopped in their tracks as they heard the name spoken by the boy. Tall, slender, with swarthy, Gallic features, they wore white planter's hats, cutaway coats, white shirts, cravats fastened bow-tie fashion, fancy vests, Eastern riding breeches and Wellington-leg boots. Each had a Western gunbelt on, the older carrying a short barreled British Webley Bulldog revolver in a cross-draw holster at his left side.

* Texans did not use the term 'cinch'.

The younger man's weapon was an Army Colt, in a low cavalry-twist rig.

First staring at the big blond, they exchanged glances and the younger opened his mouth. Before he could speak, his companion gave a vehement head-shake and strolled, with all too plainly assumed nonchalance, to the desk.

'Isn't that Captain Fog going upstairs?' the man asked, holding his voice to a level which would not reach the blond giant's ears.

'It certainly is, Mr. Corbeau,' the clerk agreed warily, watching the second of the men in case he made a hostile movement. There was something furtive about the pair's attitude which—along with them being 'scent-smelling Creole frogs'—caused him to mistrust them. 'Do you know him?'

'Not personally, although I saw him several times during the War,' the man called Corbeau replied. 'Perhaps I will pay my respects to him later.'

'I reckon he'll enjoy that,' the clerk said dryly, but Corbeau was already turning away.

Rejoining his companion, Corbeau nodded in reply to his unasked question. Then they strolled—trying to act leisurely, but with obvious haste—out of the hotel.

Watching them go, the clerk gave a disapproving sniff. From the way they had acted, Corbeau and Petain were mighty interested—and considerably put out—by seeing Captain Dusty Fog. Maybe they had locked horns with him in the War. Sure, they had most likely worn the Gray; but those Creoles had, by all accounts, done as much fighting amongst themselves as with the Yankees. Perhaps Captain Fog had had to make wolf bait of one of their kin in a duel.

Whatever the cause, Corbeau and Petain had not lingered long after seeing Captain Fog. They might, of course, be planning to come back later. The clerk wondered if he should convey a warning to the blond giant. Then he grinned and told himself that such an action would be unnecessary. Captain Fog could chill the milk of a couple of fancy-smelling Louisiana dudes, happen they got feisty, one-handed; and left-handed at that.

Unaware of the interest he had aroused in two of Los Cabestrillo's visitors, the big blond continued to climb the stairs and answered the boy's question.

'The very ones,' he confirmed, thinking with some amusement how the incident to which the boy referred had become enlarged upon and distorted.* 'Only it wasn't the *whole* Mexican Army. I heard tell that at least ten of them were on furlough at the time.'

'Folks do say that you, Mark Counter, the Ysabel Kid 'n' Waco stopped us needing to go to war 'n' ship the Greasers,' the boy went on.

'That's what they say,' the blond admitted, for the boy's words had been close to the truth.

'Who-all's the strongest, you or Mark?' asked the bellhop, studying the man's magnificent physique and recollecting various stories he had heard concerning Mark Counter's physical prowess.

''It's about even.'

'Did he for real heft ole Calamity Jane's wagon out of a gopher hole?'†

'Yep.'

'And yank the whole danged window, bars 'n' all, out of the wall of the Tennyson jail, one-handed, so's he could get out secret 'n' lick the whole blasted Cousins' gang?'‡

'He always told me he used both hands to do it,' the blond corrected.

'*You* could've done it *one*-handed,' the boy praised.

'Not *left*-handed,' the blond objected modestly. 'What's doing in town?'

'Same's every danged night,' the boy replied disgustedly. 'Nothing. You on your way to San Antone to face down Shangai Pierce and them other fellers?'

---

* Told in: THE PEACEMAKERS.

† Told in the 'The Bounty on Belle Starr's Scalp' episode of: *TROUBLED RANGE.*

‡ Told in the 'Better Than Calamity' episode of: *THE WILD-CATS.*

'I'm going to talk peace with 'em,' answered the blond.

'Happen they've got a lick of good sense 'tween 'em, they'll listen good,' the bellhop declared. 'Meeting's not for two weeks or so, is it?'

'Nope. Only I've got to visit some kin and do things before I get there.'

By that time, they had reached the door of Room Twenty-One. Showing his disappointment at having arrived so quickly, the boy unlocked and opened the door. Entering, he hurried across and turned up the light of the lamp on the dressing-table. The room was small, but neatly and cleanly furnished.

'Hope it's all right, Cap'n,' he said anxiously.

'Best I've seen this side of Mulrooney, Kansas,' the blond giant assured the boy, setting his saddle down carefully on its right side by the wall. Taking a silver dollar from his pocket, he flipped it through the air. 'Here. Don't you go spending it all on the one woman, mind.'

'*Woman!*' the boy spat disgustedly. 'You don't catch Waxahachie Smith wasting money on no woman. I'm going to put it to good use 'n' buy some powder, balls and caps for my Navy Colt.'

Having delivered the sentiment, the boy left the room. Whether the blond's tip was spent on ammunition or not, Waxahachie Smith would one day become almost as well known in gun-fighting circles as was the man who had given it to him.*

'Somebody should ought to have a long talk to that boy,' the big Texan thought, grinning, as he watched the door close behind the bellhop. 'Still, time was when I'd've figured the same way.'

Having delivered the sentiment, he removed his hat. He ran his fingers along the fancy barbiquejo and the sardonic grin changed to a gentle smile. Hanging the hat on the bed post, he sat down and took a letter from a

* How Waxahachie Smith gained and earned his fame is told in: *SLIP GUN, NO FINGER ON THE TRIGGER* and *CURE THE TEXAS FEVER.*

pocket built into the inside of his shirt. The envelope
had seen frequent handling; which might have been due
to the fact that the address was written in a neat,
feminine hand.

It said:

> MARK COUNTER,
> c/o Duke Bent,
> Bent's Ford,
> Indian Nations.

Taking out the letter, the man who had signed the
register as 'Captain D.E.M. Fog' read it with every
evidence of pleasure.

If the clerk had been in a position to witness the
scene, he might have been deeply disappointed. Apparently the man he had so admired for years, one of
Texas's most honored and respected sons, was
stooping to read a good friend's private and *very* personal mail.

Appearances are frequently deceptive.

There was a simple explanation to why the blond
giant should be reading mail addressed to 'Mark
Counter'.

That was his name.

He was not Dusty Fog!

When the Governor of Texas had been informed that
a town was acting as a safe refuge for wanted men, he
had sworn that he would cause it to be closed down.
Stanton Howard had been brought in to clean up the
mess left by Davis's corrupt, inefficient Reconstruction
Administration and the return to law and order stood
high on his list of priorities.

How to bring an end to the town—which went by the
dramatic name of Hell—had posed a problem. Even if a
Company of Texas Rangers might not have been
capable of handling the situation, Howard could have
called upon the services of the United States Army and
sent a regiment or more of cavalry to the town.

Except for one *very* significant objection.

The town was situated deep in the Palo Duro country and that was the undisputed domain of the *Kweharehnuh* Comanches. Unlike the other bands of the *Nemenuh** at the Fort Sorrel Peace Treaty meeting, the Antelopes had refused to come in to the reservation.† Retreating to their wild Palo Duro and Tule terrain, they had expressed their determination to continue living in their traditional manner.

The full story of how Mayor Lampart had obtained permission to set up his town for outlaws, and had won the active co-operation of the *Kweharehnuh* has been told elsewhere.

Briefly: one of the prices he had paid for the privilege had been to give every Antelope brave-heart a repeating rifle and a regular, but not excessive, supply of ammunition.

To send in soldiers armed with single-shot Springfield carbines—even if they were given the backing of artillery—would have meant a long, hard campaign and a high cost in lives. Fighting over terrain which they knew as well as the backs of their hands, all the advantages would have been with the Comanches. What was more, once the fighting started, it might spread to and involve the warriors living restlessly at peace on the reservations.

Howard had decided to dispatch a small party to scout out the situation. Using members of the Texas Rangers had been considered unwise, if not downright precarious. With wanted men from all over Texas likely to be in town, the risk of the peace officers being recognized as such could not be ignored. What had been needed were men with courage, gun skill, initiative and intelligence; but who were less likely to be known by outlaws.

That had been where Dusty Fog had come in. His experience as a peace officer had been in Kansas, or Montana, and he had all the other qualities. Enough, at any

* Nemenuh: 'The People', the Comanches' name for their nation.

† The reason that the Kweharehnuh did not come in is told in: *SIDEWINDER*.

rate, to give him an even chance of survival. However, before he would agree to take in his companions, the Ysabel Kid and Waco, Dusty had insisted that they were given an elaborate, but thorough cover story. At his instigation, the stories of the Paymaster's robbery and the Governor's arbitration for the quarreling ranchers had been circulated.*

Instead of accompanying his *amigos*, Mark Counter had been given an equally important—if more passive—role. That did not imply a lack of faith in his courage, intelligence, initiative or abilities.

The youngest son of a wealthy Big Bend rancher, Mark had accepted Dusty's offer of employment as being more likely to lead to adventure, excitement and fun than working on his father's spread. Master of every branch of the cowhand's trade, famous for his prowess in a roughhouse brawl and by virtue of his enormous physical strength, he was known as Dusty Fog's right bower. Living as he did in the shadow of the Rio Hondo gun wizard, Mark's true potential as a gunfighter had received small acclaim. People in the position to make a judgment declared that he was second only to Dusty Fog in the matter of speed and accuracy.

Mark's role in the deception had stemmed from the fact that he looked like most people imagined a man of Dusty Fog's legendary reputation would be. So he was traveling by an indirect route to San Antonio de Bexar, where he would post as the OD Connected's segundo when the Governor held the peace-keeping talks.

From information he had received, Howard had warned that the townspeople of Hell had reliable sources of information and effective means of obtaining news from more civilized areas. So it had been decided, with the ranchers in question's co-operation, that the

* While Belle Boyd had drawn the correct conclusions from the two stories, that the 'Caxton brothers' and 'Comanche Blood' were Dusty Fog and his amigos, she had misinterpreted the nature of their mission. They were not hunting for the Brotherhood For Southron Freedom.

meeting must take place as announced. Nobody could have been sure how long Dusty's mission would take. The Governor had been determined to do everything in his power to keep up the pretense which might save the three young Texans' lives.

Taking the letter from its envelope, Mark smoothed and read its familiar words. It was written by lady outlaw Belle Starr, with whom he was on close—and occasionally initimate—terms.* She had sent it to Bent's Ford, knowing that Mark would be coming by the place on his way home from a trial drive. In addition to a warm, tender message, she had enclosed the plaited leather *barbiquejo*.

'That Belle sure is a loving gal,' Mark told himself, having re-read and returned the letter to his shirt's pocket. 'A man could do worse than marry her. Trouble being, I'm not the marrying kind—and neither is she.'

* How Mark's association with Belle Starr began, developed and finally ended is told in: *TROUBLED RANGE, RANGELAND HERCULES*, the 'A Lady Known As Belle' episode of *THE TEXAN, THE BAD BUNCH* and *GUNS IN THE NIGHT*.

CHAPTER SEVEN

I Don't Like Stinking Rebs!

Mark Counter's arrival in the barroom of the Longhorn Hotel attracted considerable attention. Having found the dining-room empty, he was meaning to do no more than inquire if he could be served with a meal. Finding so many of the local citizens present, he decided that he might as well establish the fact that 'Captain Dusty Fog' was in Los Cabestrillo. Gathered in by the reports which the desk clerk and the bellhop had spread, almost every male member of the community sat or stood in the room. There was an anticipatory hush as the blond giant made his way to the counter.

'Good evening, Captain Fog,' the bartender greeted, loud enough to ensure that none of his customers would be left in doubt as to the giant Texan's indentity. 'What can I get you?'

'A meal would go down right well,' Mark replied. 'My cooking's not what it used to be. It's got a whole lot worse.'

'I'll have the cook make you up a meal,' the bartender offered, after having laughed immoderately at the comment. 'Dining-room's closed by rights, but I figure we can do something for *you*. Is there anything else I can get for you while you're waiting?'

'Whiskey, four fingers for me and set up drinks for these gents,' Mark answered. To himself, silently, he went on, 'I sure hope Governor Howard can explain away all the money I've spent like this, making folks remember ole Dusty's been to town.'

There was a modest swarm for the bar. Nobody wished to appear greedy, but had an equal objection to allowing others a better chance of making the acquaintance of their illustrious visitor. However, they soon found that 'Cap'n Fog's' desire for hard liquor was not extensive. Finishing his drink and another set up by the bartender, the blond giant announced that he would not be drinking any more.

'Not on an empty stomach, gents,' Mark apologized. 'Anyways, I've been in the saddle since sun-up and I'm fixing to make an early start come morning. So I'll say, "Thank you, but no more." And we'll let it go at that.'

Even if they felt disappointed at losing the opportunity of a lengthy drinking and yarning session with 'Dusty Fog', nobody displayed an inclination to dispute his right to decline further hospitality.

Strolling out of the barroom, Mark crossed the hall. A smiling Mexican waiter stood by a table in the otherwise deserted dining-room and indicated the place which he had just set.

'The food won't be long, *senor*,' the waiter declared as Mark sat down.

Mark still had the room to himself when he reached the coffee stage of his meal. Nor did he feel any particular need for company. Especially of the kind which arrived.

Barged in would have been a better term.

Stamping truculently with their heavy, Wellington-leg Jefferson boots, two big, brawny soldiers came into the dining-room. They wore the usual Burnside campaign hats, blue tunics, riding breeches with yellow stripes along the outside seams, and accoutrements of the United States Cavalry. The brass buttons were dulled, the clothing and leather work dirty. One was a corporal, with a tawny stubble of whiskers on his surly face. The other, an enlisted man, was also unshaven and his features had a slightly Mongoloid look. Neither was

sober, and they gave the impression of having taken
enough to drink to make them dangerous.

'It's too late to get a meal, *senores*,' the waiter
warned politely.

'Like hell it is!' growled the corporal. 'Me 'n' Jan
here've rid a long ways and wants feeding.'

'We being here to protect you lousy Rebs from In-
juns, and all, you owe us that,' Jan went on, his accent
indicative of Mid-European upbringing. 'So you just get
to it.'

While talking, the two slouched towards Mark's
table. He watched them with no great interest and concern. Dirty, drunken soldiers were not sufficient of a
novelty to warrant his attention. Unless, of course, their
behavior provided him with a reason.

'The cook's gone home——,' the waiter began.

'You've fed the beef-head here,' the corporal pointed
out, jerking a thumb in the big blond's direction. 'So
now you can feed us.'

No Texan took to being called a beef-head, which was
the derogatory name applied to them by Kansans who
wished to be insulting. So the man's behavior looked
like causing Mark to take an interest in him.

'I don't like stinking Rebs!' Jan declared, standing
slightly to one side and behind the non-com, as he
thumbed open the flap of his holster.

Taken with the comment, the solider's action drew
Mark's eyes in his direction. Almost as if following a
preconceived plan, the corporal took a step closer. His
big hands hooked up under the edge of Mark's table and
started to lift.

Realizing his mistake, the big blond tried to thrust
back his chair and rise. Under the corporal's
propulsion, the table elevated and tilted. The coffee cup
slid from it, followed by the cruet and sugar-bowl,
cascading into Mark's lap. Coming downwards, the
nearest edge of the table caught him on the thighs before
he could get clear. Pain caused him to jerk rearwards,
slamming his rump on to the chair's seat. Unable to take

the strain, the rear legs snapped and precipitated him backwards.

Watching Mark going down, Jan grinned and lunged forward. The soldier planned to stamp on the center of the Texan's chest as soon as he hit the floor. An attack of that kind would render him practically helpless and wide open to anything further the two men wished to do.

Years of horse-riding experience had taught Mark how to fall, even unexpectedly and backwards, with the best chance of alighting safely. So, although he could not prevent himself going down, he managed to break his fall with his hands on arrival.

Looming over what he assumed was a winded, incapacitated victim, Jan put his plan into action. Balancing on his left foot, he raised and bent the right leg. Down it drove, but did not reach its target. Two hands, which felt more like the crushing jaws of a bear-trap, clamped hold of the descending boot and halted it.

Having made his catch, Mark proceeded to make the most of it. Thrusting himself into the sitting position, he gave a twisting heave at the trapped boot. Jan felt as if his leg was being turned into a corkscrew. Then he was thrust with irresistible force and sent sprawling wildly across the room.

After tipping over the table, the corporal made as if to advance and join Jan in assaulting the big blond. Showing courage, the little waiter yelped a protest and grabbed the non-com's arms. Small and slight of build, the Mexican lacked the strength to do more than delay the burly two-bar. However, by doing so, he gave Mark the opportunity to attend to the trooper's attack.

And caused the corporal to make a hurried revision of his plans.

With a snarl, the bulky non-com wrenched himself free and sent the waiter staggering. At which instant, he observed Jan going away helplessly from Mark's counter to the attack.

Swiftly the non-com reviewed the situation and formed his conclusions.

Sure, he almost equaled the blond giant in height. Being more thick-set, he probably had an edge in weight. He had the benefit of being on his feet, against a seated opponent.

All good, sound advantages which boded well for a successful assault.

Except when the opponent in question was 'Dusty Fog'!

There were far too many stories told, concerning the Rio Hondo gun wizard's equally magical ability to protect himself with his bare hands, for the corporal to be enamored with the idea of fighting in that fashion.

Most men, treated as 'Fog' had been, would have been winded and helpless after such a fall. That big, blond bastard had not only broken the force of the impact, he had done it quickly enough to let him stave off Jan's attempt at caving in his chest.

A man with such ability would be anything but easy meat in a brawl.

So, no matter how *they* wanted things playing, the plan must be changed.

No matter that he had shown considerable sympathy for the Yankees since the end of the War, 'Fog' would not let their blue uniforms stop him taking severe measures to protect himself. He looked strong enough to have duplicated Mark Counter's trick of ripping out the bars at the Tennyson jail; and doing it one-handed.

Bearing that in mind, displaying a speed which implied long experience with the awkward rig United States—and many Johnny Reb's—soldiers were compelled to use, the corporal thumbed free the flap of his holster. Hs right hand twisted, grasping the butt and snaking the revolver from leather. Cocking back the hammer, he turned the muzzle in Mark's direction.

Seeing his danger, the blond giant realized its full, deadly potential. Joe Gaylin, the El Paso leather worker, had designed Mark's holsters for security of their weapons, comfort during hours of wear and ease in allowing the Colts to be drawn. However, the seven-and-a-half-inch lengths of the Cavalry Model Peacemakers did not lend themselves to a fast draw when seated.

Even as Mark's right fingers enfolded the ivory butt, he knew that he would be too late. Maybe he could throw himself aside and avoid the corporal's first shot, but a second must surely find his body before he could make a positive response. As if that was not enough, Jan had collided with the wall rump-to-timber. He was glaring in Mark's direction and duplicating the non-com's actions with regard to continuing the fight.

Even as death stared Mark in the face, a shot rang out. It was the deep, distinctive sound of a heavy-calibre, short-barreled revolver. Fired from the doorway, the bullet took the corporal in the head. He was twirled around by the impact and the revolver tumbled from his lifeless hand.

Wanting to discover who had saved his life, Mark flickered a glance across the room. Guns in hand, the two Creole dudes he had noticed earlier had rushed from the hall. Smoke curled from the Webley Bulldog in the hands of the elder. Gripping his cocked Army Colt, the younger man swung immediately in Jan's direction. It was almost as if he had known just where to look for the trooper.

Although Jan had completed his draw, he ignored the new arrivals in his determination to be avenged upon Mark. Then he seemed to become aware that one of the pair was forming a threat to his well-being.

Skidding to a halt, the younger Creole started to raise his weapons to shoulder-height. Extending the revolver at arm's length, as leisurely as if he was taking part in a formal duel with no especial need for haste, he took careful and deliberate aim.

As if suddenly becoming aware of Petain's actions, Jan swung his head around. He stared, almost registering disbelief at what he saw, and his revolver wavered instead of aligning itself on Mark. The trooper opened his mouth, but was not granted the opportunity to speak.

Having made certain of his aim—in a way which

would have proved fatal under Western gunfight conditions—Petain squeezed the Colt's trigger. Flame
lashed from the muzzle and powder smoke swirled
briefly. A .44 of an inch hole appeared just over Jan's
left eyebrow. Then blood, brains and slivers of shattered bone sprayed onto the wall as the bullet burst out
of his skull. Down Jan slid, as if he had been boned, the
revolver clattering by his side.

'Are you all right, Captain Fog?' Corbeau asked
solicitously, walking forward with the revolver
dangling in his hand.

'I am now,' Mark admitted, standing up. 'Thanks,
mister.'

'No thanks are necessary, sir,' Corbeau declared. 'We
Southrons should stick together and be willing to help
each other.'

Before any more could be said, there was a com-
motion in the hall. Attracted by the disturbance, the occupants of the barroom came streaming in. Crowding
forward, they stared about them and all seemed to be
speaking at the same time.

'What happened?'

'Why'd they jump you, Cap'n Fog?'

'Where's the marshal?'

'It must be some of them blue-bellies who've been
causing all the fuss around 'n' about!'

'Where the hell did them two come from?'

'Gentlemen! Please!' Corbeau shouted, facing the
thickest portion of the crowd and waving his left hand
in a signal for silence. 'Can we please have a little
order?'

Slowly the chatter died away and the new arrivals
waited expectantly for the next development.

'Somebody'd best go and fetch the marshal,' Mark
suggested, having failed to locate that official amongst
the townsmen. 'And I'd be obliged if most of you'll go
back to the bar until we've talked this thing out.'

Glaring coldly about him, as he had seen Dusty do
when determined to enforce an unpopular decision or
command, Mark brought about the desired effect.

Slowly, with every evidence of reluctance, the citizens retreated into the entrance lobby. There, they asserted their independence by hovering around and straining their ears to hear what was being said in the dining-room.

'You gents came just in time,' Mark drawled, after his request had been fulfilled. 'I'm obliged.'

"It was our pleasure to help, sir,' Corbeau insisted, returning the Webley to its holster. 'We were just passing when we heard them abusing you. Knowing how Yankees stand by their own, we thought that you might care for witnesses who could testify that the provocation was on their part.'

'When we saw your danger,' Petain went on, sliding away his Colt. 'We knew that we would have to take more positive steps to help.'

'I wouldn't have said "no" if you'd asked before cutting in,' Mark stated. 'But I didn't know that there was a military post near here.'

'There's a detachment, about a company, not far away,' Corbeau replied. 'Or so I've been told. Apparently its commanding officer doesn't take to having Southron visitors.'

'His men have been getting into fights and generally raising hell in the surrounding counties,' Petain enlarged. 'So far, though, they've left Los Cabestrillo alone.'

Mark was puzzled by the words. News traveled fast, surprisingly so, across the Texas range country. Yet he could not recollect having heard of trouble being caused by soldiers. Not recently, at any rate. Shortly after the War, there had been incidents in plenty. With the passing of time, however, reasonably friendly relations had returned.

There were, of course, soldiers—and civilians—who refused to accept that the War had ended. Mark's late assailants had looked like the kind of men who would fall into that category.

Further conversation was ended by the arrival of the

town marshal. Looking at him, Mark decided that Los Cabestrillo's city fathers went in for economy rather than efficiency in their law enforcement. Big, pot-bellied, clad in old town clothes, Marshal Flatter—a remarkably inappropriate name—looked, moved and spoke in a lethargic manner.

Staring around him myopically, Flatter asked to be told what had 'come off in here?'

While Corbeau started to give the Creoles' version, Mark found his attention straying to the corporal's body. The blond giant wondered why the two men had made their unprovoked attack. Hatred for Johnny Rebs might have accounted for it, yet that seemed a mighty flimsy reason for trying to kill him. If the two dudes had not intervened, it might easily have come to that.

One thing was for sure. No matter how great his antipathy towards Southrons, the soldiers' commanding officer could hardly substantiate a claim that they had been killed without good reason. Each had drawn his revolver with the intention of using it. The weapons lay by their sides——

Walking to the corporal's body, Mark bent to take up the revolver. At first glance, it looked like an 1851 Navy Colt. That was unusual. Not because the weapon in question was cap-and-ball fired; the Army had not yet equipped every regiment with metallic cartridge revolvers. The U.S. Cavalry had, however, standardized its armament by supplying the *1860 Army* Colt.

Occasionally men purchased their own sidearms, but the pair did not strike Mark as being so keen that they would have done so. And even if they had——

The revolver's frame was brass, instead of the usual steel!

No Colt had ever been manufactured in such a fashion!

Frowning, Mark lifted the weapon and read the inscription along the top of the octagonal barrel.

'SCHNEIDER & GLASSWICK, MEMPHIS, TENN.'

'Do you-all know why they jumped you, Cap'n Fog?'

Although Mark heard the words, they did not register immediately as having been addressed to him.

'Do you know them from somewhere?' Petain supplemented, when the big Texan did not answer Flatter's question.

'I can't place them,' Mark admitted, putting the revolver down and turning to face the men. 'Anyways, I don't think that they jumped me because of who I am——.'

'Just because you are a Southron,' Corbeau finished for Mark, speaking in a louder voice than was necessary.

The words clearly had carried to the listening men in the hall, for a low rumble of talk rose in their wake. Indignation filled the voices of the eavesdropping citizens, at the attempt by Yankee soldiers upon the life of the town's distinguished visitor—perhaps merely because he was a Southron.

'They were drunk,' Mark began. 'Likely just mean and looking for a fight.'

'More'n that, I'd say,' Flatter injected, trying to look wise. 'If these gents hadn't cut in, they'd've gunned you down without a chance.'

''Somebody ought to do something about it!' Petain growled angrily. 'These damned Yankees think that they can come rampaging through Southern towns, terrorizing the women and endangering lives with impunity.'

'What're you fixing to do about it, Flattie?' demanded an indignant voice from the hall.

'Well now,' the marshal answered, scratching his head. 'I don't rightly see's how I can do anything. Can't arrest 'em, for sure, them being dead 'n' all.'

'Their blasted officer ain't dead!' the speaker from the hall pointed out.

'And he ain't in town, neither, so far's I know,' Flatter countered. 'Nor camped in Kendal County. Which means he ain't in my juri—jurification.'

'You'll have to make sure that he knows you hold him

responsible for what happened, marshal,' Corbeau warned. '*That* is in your jurisdiction.'

'I ain't rightly sure I knows where to look for him,' Flatter complained.

'Maybe they're carrying something that'll tell us where they're from,'' Mark suggested, kneeling and reaching towards the pocket of the corporal's tunic.

The tarnished brass buttons differed in two respects from those normally worn by members of the United States Army. Firstly, they bore a letter 'D' and not the 'A', 'I' or 'C'—Artillery, Infantry, Cavalry—by which the wearer's arm of the service could be recognized. Secondly, encircling the embossed spread-eagle on a three-pointed shield device, were the words, '*AD ASTRA PER ASPERA*'.

Mark knew that the words were the motto of the Sovereign State of Kansas.

At one time, the 'D' would have announced that the man sporting the button so inscribed was a Dragoon.

Although in the early days of the War the Yankees had permitted the various States, and other patriotic bodies, to arm and equip volunteer regiments in any way they had chosen, Congress had eventually insisted upon standardization of uniforms. At about the same time, the terms like 'Dragoon', 'Lancer', 'Hussar' and '*Chasseurs*'—which had graced the volunteer regiments—had been superceded by the more prosaic 'Cavalry', regardless of the outfit's composition and characteristics.

So why was a cavalryman, in 1874, still wearing the buttons of what must have been a Kansas volunteer regiment of Dragoons?

Perhaps he had been so proud of his home State, and old outfit, that he was willing to flout *Dress Regulations* and wear the means of displaying his loyalty to both.

Even if that should have been the case, it did not explain why he was armed with a revolver which had been manufactured in a Confederate States' firearms' factory.

CHAPTER EIGHT

That's Mark Counter

Holding their horses to a steady trot, Mark Counter, Louis Corbeau and Paul Petain rode through the starlit darkness towards where, half a mile away, the lights of a building flickered intermittently through gaps in a large clump of post oaks.

'You understand, of course, Captain Fog, that I'm telling you this in all confidence.' Corbeau warned solemnly. 'And that I expect you, as an officer of the Confederate States Army, and a Southern gentleman, to respect this confidence.'

'I understand,' Mark answered.

'And that, whatever action General Hardin decides upon,' Corbeau continued, 'he will be discreet.'

'O—Uncle Devil's always discreet,' Mark declared. 'And, like I said, it's his decision on what we do. I'll go along with him. It may take him some hard thinking, but he'll send you an answer, count on it.'

Some instinct, for which he had subsequently been grateful, had warned the blond giant against commenting upon the dead corporal's buttons and weapon. To add to his puzzlement, Mark had found that Jan sported similar buttons and carried a Confederate Leech & Rigdon Army revolver.

Although the task should have been performed by the marshal, Mark had taken it upon himself to search both bodies. He had found neither document nor clue to their identity, nor anything to suggest to which regiment they belonged. Even more surprising, if they should have been visiting the town for recreational purposes, their pockets had been equally devoid of money.

On the latter point, Petain had stated—speaking in tones loud enough to reach the listening men in the hall—that the pair had probably believed their blue Yankee uniforms were all the currency they would need when dealing with Southron businessmen. At the time, Mark had put the comment down to having come from an embittered young hot-head who refused to accept that the War had ended in 'Sixty-Five.

If Flatter had seen and drawn any conclusions from the puzzling aspects, he had successfully kept them to himself. Mark was inclined to believe that the marshal had not noticed either factor; but was taking everything at its face value, to make sure that he did not embarrass his town's distinguished visitor.

Pressed for a comment on what he was planning to do next, Flatter had declared that it was his intention to telegraph the County Sheriff in Boerne and turn the matter over to that official. When Mark had asked if he would be required for a hearing into the incident, Flatter had grown even more vague. Finally, the blond giant had taken pity on the peace officer and had promised that he would remain in Los Cabestrillo until the sheriff arrived from the County seat.

Compassion for the bumbling, incompetent marshal had not been Mark's sole motive. The big blond had sensed that some connection might exist between his attackers and the men whose timely arrival had saved his life.

There had been at least two pointers in that direction. While the soldiers had been drinking and had certainly been on the prod, they had seemed to be making a predetermined rather than a spontaneous attack. When the Creoles had made their presence known, Jan had not reacted in the manner which Mark would have expected. Instead of turning immediately, to discover who had shot his companion, the trooper had continued to devote his attention to the giant Texan.

It had almost been as if Jan believed there was

nothing to fear from the newcomers. Not until Petain
had taken a deliberate aim at him had Jan shown any
realization of his peril; and then it had been too late.

If the Creoles were connected in some way with the
soldiers, why had they saved Mark's life?

Could it have been because they had very strong
reasons for wishing to place 'Dusty Fog'—for it was he
whom they had assumed Mark to be—into their debt?

That was possible.

The Rio Hondo gun wizard was famous for standing
by his friends and always repaying favors. Without a
doubt, he would have been grateful to men who had
saved his life and willing to help them in return.

If Mark's theory should have been correct, it had implied that the Creoles had most likely arranged for the
soldiers to attack him. They must have had a mighty
powerful reason for taking such a dangerous and
desperate step. Sufficiently so for Mark to have decided
that he wanted to know what it might be.

Arranging the means by which he could satisfy his
curiosity had not been difficult. In fact, doing it had
been taken out of his hands completely.

After the marshal had concluded what had satisfied
him as a detailed and instructive inquiry into the affair,
he had allowed the three men concerned to go about
their business. Knowing that he would learn nothing
more from that source, Mark had left Flatter to dispose
of the bodies. At Corbeau's invitation, he had accompanied the Creoles into the barroom and had done
the honors at the counter.

Once they had obtained their drinks, Corbeau had
left Petain to divert the other occupants of the room by
a description of the fight with the *Yankee* soldiers.
Mark had noticed how the young dude had laid great
emphasis on the word 'Yankee', but had put it down to
the same motives as had inspired his comment on the
dead men's lack of money.

Taking Mark aside, Corbeau had asked if he would
accompany them—Petain and himself—to the ranch of
a friend which lay some five miles outside the town.

Mark had discarded the idea that they might be planning to lure him away and kill him. If they had merely wanted him killed, they would have allowed the soldiers to do the job, shooting the pair down in such a way that it would have seemed they were just too late to prevent 'Captain Fog's' death.

Robbery might have been their motive, but Mark doubted it. While it might have been assumed that the segundo of the OD Connected would not be traveling with empty pockets, he also would not be likely to carry sufficient money to make such an elaborate plot worth trying.

Concluding that he would lose nothing by going along, Mark had given his consent. He had pointed out that his trousers were soaked with coffee and had gone to his room to change them for a dry pair. Collecting his hat and saddle, leaving the bed roll behind, he had returned to the barroom. On entering, he had found the crowd in a kind of mood such as he had not seen since the earliest and worst days of Reconstruction.

Curses were being directed from all sides at the United States and men had been recounting tales of Yankee atrocities, before, during and since the War. Mark had hoped that no more soldiers would arrive. The sight of a blue uniform might easily have led to a lynching, or open conflict, and Marshal Flatter was not the kind of peace officer who would control such a situation.

Sensing that the Creoles, particularly Petain, had been responsible for the crowd's mood, Mark had been grateful for his decision to accompany them to their friends' ranch. He had wasted no time in getting them out of the hotel.

Collecting their horses from the livery barn, the two men had guided Mark from the town and across the range. At no time did either of them act in a manner which suggested that they might have been contemplating a robbery. Within five minutes, Mark had lost all apprehensions on that account; and had known, or detected what might have been, a reason for his 'rescue'.

Corbeau had done most of the talking. First he had reminded Mark of the worst attributes of Reconstruction; including how his—Dusty Fog's—cousin, John Wesley Hardin, had been turned from a happy-go-lucky cowhand into a wanted killer through the oppression of Yankee carpetbagger officials.* Then he had told how the Brotherhood For Southron Freedom had been formed and planned to bring an end to the Union's tyranny. When the time was right, the South would rise again.

Until then, there were preparations to be made.

What the Brotherhood needed was men—and leaders. Already Colonel Anton de Richelieu was gathering the nucleus of a new Confederate States Army. When the day of reckoning came, a European country—Corbeau had tactfully refused to say which one—would pour arms, supplies and money into the South.

Would Captain Fog be interested in taking his place amongst the ranks of the Confederate States liberators?

Could the Brotherhood For Southern Freedom count upon General Ole Devil Hardin's support and blessing?

If the answer to both the questions should be in the affirmative, Corbeau had claimed—and Mark had known it to be true—then most of Texas would flock to the Stars and Bars battle flag of the reborn Confederate States.

Revising his first inclination to refuse, Mark had decided to make a pretense of interest and possible acquiescence. He had wanted to know more about the Brotherhood and felt certain that his boss would be most interested; although probably not in a manner that would meet with its members' approval.

So Mark had stated that, while he could not answer for his 'Uncle Devil's' sentiments, he felt sure that they would be suitable. He had also warned that his own participation would depend upon how Ole Devil decided to act.

Although that had apparently satisfied Corbeau and

* Told in: *THE HOODED RIDERS.*

brought a warning of the need for discretion, Petain showed how he believed a more positive response should have been forthcoming.

'I can't see why there should be any hesitation,' the young Creole growled, 'You *are* Southerners——.'

'And damned proud of it,' Mark interrupted. 'But this isn't a small thing, *mister*. Uncle Devil will need time to consider it.'

Apparently Petain had learned that if a Texan said 'mister' after being introduced, it implied he did not like the person to whom he addressed the word. An angry scowl flickered across his handsome features as Mark said it.

'Some would say it should need no consideration,' the young Creole snapped.

'*Some* would say that a Spanish ring bit's damned cruel and unnecessary, happen a man can handle his horse,' Mark countered.

Nothing the blond giant had seen of Petain had led him to form a liking for the other. There was an air of superior, condescending, arrogant snobbishness about the Creole which ruffled the Texan's normally even temper. At the livery barn, Petain had been far rougher than was necessary in his handling and saddling of the horse. Since then, he had ridden with a strict control over the animal's movements; backing his imperious will with spurs and the use of the big, fancy Spanish ring bit. The latter device, with a metal circle that slipped over the horse's lower jaw, had always been regarded as unduly severe by Texas cowhands. In skilled hands, it could be comparatively harmless and effective; or punishing and cruel. From what Mark had seen, the Creole lacked the necessary ability to render the bit harmless. Nor would he, the big blond suspected, have been inclined to use it in a harmless manner.

'Just what are you implying?' Petain spat out, a dull red flush creeping into his cheeks.

'I figured I was just making talk,' Mark replied. 'The same as you.'

'I take your remark as a personal affront——,' Petain began heatedly.

'Take it any way you want, *mister*,' Mark drawled. 'Only you'd best mind one thing. This isn't Louisiana. In Texas, we settle our affairs-of-honor differently. There's no waiting until dawn. It's finished right then, on the spot, fast and permanently.'

'*Gentlemen!*' Corbeau barked, reining his mount around and forcing it between the other two animals. 'Our Cause is too important for us to let private differences come between us. Captain Fog meant no offense, *Captain* Petain.'

'With respect to the major,' Petain answered, bristling with indignation. 'I don't see it in that light.'

Suddenly Mark saw the reason for the young Creole's animosity. Clearly Petain took the Brotherhood For Southron Freedom's military status very seriously. He was proud to hold officer's rank in the proposed new Army of the Confederate States. So he had taken exception to Mark's use of the word 'mister'. In the Army, that was the term applied to 1st or 2nd lieutenants. A captain was accorded his correct title.

Knowing that the affair was being caused by a misunderstanding did not make the blond giant like Petain any better. However, Mark figured that he had best avoid locking horns head on with the young Creole at that time. To kill one of its senior members would not make the Brotherhood feel inclined to show him their secrets.

'My apologies for saying "*mister*", Captain Petain,' Mark said formally. 'I didn't know.'

'Well, Captain Petain?' Corbeau challenged, when the young Creole did not make a reply.

'You cast doubts as to my ability as a horseman, Captain Fog,' Petain complained, unwilling to let the affair slide by without a further gesture.

'I didn't care for your remarks concerning General Hardin's and my loyalty to the South,' Mark pointed out. 'However, if you'll withdraw your comment, I'll take mine back.'

'All right!' Petain growled grudgingly, after a pause in which Corbeau had glared angrily at him. 'I withdraw it.'

'So do I,' Mark drawled.

Although the big blond had averted a clash with the Creole, he also knew that he had made an unforgiving enemy. Reared in the school of the *code duello*, Petain would never forget that he had been forced to back down and deprived of an opportunity to demand satisfaction for a grievance.

Having continued to ride as they talked, the men were approaching the edge of the post oaks. Mark could see that Petain was darting glances around as if expecting something, or somebody. Whatever, or whoever, it was did not materialize. An angry snorting snarl broke from the younger Creole as they emerged beyond the clump and into their first clear sight of the ranch's head-quarters.

Lights showed at the windows of the big, plank-built, two story main house, through the open double doors of the barn and outside the three-holer back-house. The long one-floor adobe cabin which most likely served as a combined cook- and bunkhouse was unilluminated, as were the three pole corrals and other structures.

'Where're all your men?' Mark inquired, for the premises before him could hardly have housed over a hundred would-be soldiers.

'A few use the bunkhouse,' Corbeau answered. 'But the main body are camped in a valley beyond the post oaks.'

'We don't want anybody to see them,' Petain went on. 'So we keep them away from the ranch house. There are pickets and vedettes all round. It's impossible for any unauthorized person to get near the camp by day, or night.'

'We've done it,' the big blond pointed out.

'Only because we were expected,' Petain answered, looking uneasy.

'*Three* of us?' Mark queried.

'The vedette recognized Major Corbeau and I,' Petain growled.

'Or he was asleep,' Mark suggested.

'By God!' Petain snarled, glaring behind him. 'I'd——.'

'He probably recognized us,' Corbeau said soothingly.

Leading the way to the barn, Corbeau told Mark that he could make use of an empty stall. The men cared for their horses, with Petain muttering and glowering repeatedly into the darkness of the post oaks. At last, with the work done, the young Creole set his hat on firmly and stalked towards the door.

'I'll just take a stroll,' Petain announced, trying to sound casual, and swaggered nonchalantly from the building.

'I hope that vedette isn't asleep,' Corbeau remarked to the big blond. 'If Petain catches him, he'll wish he'd never been born. He's a mean, evil-tempered young hothead.'

'He sounds that way,' Mark said dryly. 'Happen it'll kill him one of these days, he keeps it going.'

Taking Mark across to the main house, Corbeau opened the front foor and escorted him into the hall. Voices sounded from one of the rooms which led off from the hallway and Corbeau looked at it.

'Will you wait here for a moment, please, Captain Fog?'

'Why sure,' Mark agreed.

Striding to the door, Corbeau passed out of the big blond's sight. Mark tried to see into the room, but failed. He was not kept in suspense for long. Returning to the hall, Corbeau signaled for him to come forward. Clearly the Creole intended to make as big an impression as possible and show off his find in an impressive manner.

'Gentlemen,' Corbeau announced, standing aside for the blond giant to precede him. 'May I present Captain Dustine Edward Marsden Fog, Company 'C', Texas Light Cavalry.'

Strolling into the large, comfortable, if functionally, furnished combination library-study, Mark was confronted by half a dozen men gathered at a polish-topped table. Four of them wore the uniforms of Confederate States Army Officers and were, the blond noticed with relief, strangers.

Unfortunately, that happy state did not apply to the other two.

Dressed in range clothing belting low-tied Army Colts, they were all too familiar to Mark; despite the fact that they had not met for several years.

One thing was for certain sure.

Maybe the four officers would accept Mark as the genuine article. But Cal Roxby and Saul Brown had good cause to know that he was not Dusty Fog.

While handling an assignment unaccompanied by the other members of the floating outfit,* Mark had locked horns with the two men. A pair of hired gunfighters, they had been in the process of bullying a rancher and his wife when the big blond had intervened. Disarming them, he had handed the woman his own weapons and delivered a beating which neither would be likely to have forgotten. Then he had turned them over to the local sheriff and had last seen them, screaming threats of vengeance against him, on their way to the State's Penitentiary.

Apparently they had served their sentences and been released. Mark doubted if that would have made them feel any better disposed towards him.

'You stupid bastards!' yelled Roxby, as he and his companion sprang from the table with hands diving towards guns. 'That's Mark Counter, not Dusty Fog!'

Having expected such a reaction, Mark dipped his right hand in a sight-defying motion. The off-side long-barreled Peacemaker flowed from its holster, lined and fired. Before Roxby's revolver had cleared leather, the

---

* Floating outfit: four to six cowhands employed by a large ranch to work its more distant ranges independently, instead of being based at the main house. Ole Devil Hardin's floating outfit also acted as trouble-shooters for any of his friends who required their services.

blond giant's bullet was tearing into his chest. Cocking the Colt on its recoil, Mark turned it and cut loose at the second outlaw. Already the man's weapon was lifted into alignment. Struck by the flying lead, his body jerked violently and his own load winged harmlessly into the door.

Although he had taken the two men out of the deal, Mark knew that he was a long ways from being out of the tall timber. Every other man in the room was rising and commencing his draw. The blond giant knew that he could not hope to stop them all.

CHAPTER NINE

Whip My Soldiers Into Shape

Even when Mark Counter prepared to sell his life dearly, and brought out his lefthand Colt to make the price still higher, he heard the room's second door being thrown open.

'Attention!' barked a crisp, authoritative voice which sounded vaguely, yet positively, familiar to the blond giant's ears.

While the four confronting Mark did not go to the extent of assuming correct military braces, they at least refrained from completing their draws. For his part, the big Texan kept the matched Colts lined. Their hammers were held at full cock by his thumbs, and his forefingers depressed the triggers. Instead of taking any further action, he turned to gaze at another figure from his past.

Tall, lean as a steer raised in the greasewood thickets, the man in the doorway looked little different to when Mark had last seen him. He still wore an immaculately-fitting Confederate States Cavalry officer's undress uniform. But, where there had only been a single major's insignia on his stand-up collar, he now sported the three gold stars of a full colonel.

Maybe the face was more lined than in the days when Major Byron Aspley had commanded Mark's Company of Bushrod Sheldon's 18th Cavalry Regiment. It was still the same hard, tanned, expressionless mask, with cold brown eyes, a straight nose and tight, thin lips that never seemed to smile. Bare-headed, he had a mass of long black hair, carefully combed to conceal his ears.

Except that Mark knew there was no ear on the left side.

It had been lost, during the War, while Aspley had been saving the big blond's life.

'What's all this, Major Corbeau?' the man Mark had known as Byron Aspley demanded, striding forward as stiff-backed and smart as if he had been approaching General Robert E. Lee.

'This—he told me he was Captain Fog, Colonel,' Corbeau spluttered, standing slightly behind and to Mark's rear. 'Roxby and Brown said he was Mark Counter, then tried to kill him.'

'It seems you haven't lost your dexterity with your hand-guns, Mr. Counter,' Aspley commented. 'You can holster them now.'

'Could be I might need them again, Maj—Colonel Aspley,' Mark drawled.

'Not "Aspley"!' the lean man snapped. 'I renounced my birthright after the shameful surrender at the Appomattox Courthouse. Until the South regains its freedom, I will go by the name "de Richelieu".'

'I see, sir,' Mark drawled, and meant what he said.

De Richelieu's home, the magnificent Aspley Manor, had been one of the properties to suffer from the ravages of Sherman's 'March To The Sea'. It had been reduced to ashes and, attempting to save something from the burning rooms, his parents had died in the conflagration. Learning of this, Aspley had become obsessed with a deep, bitter hatred for the Yankees. He had raged furiously over General Lee's surrender; and was a prime mover in the scheme to offer Sheldon's Regiment to the French's self-appointed ruler of Mexico. Aspley alone had elected to remain in Maximilian's service when Dusty Fog had delivered President U.S. Grant's message requesting that the Regiment return to their homes.*

Having helped Dusty—it had been then that they had had their first meeting—Mark had sometimes wondered

---

* Told in: *THE YSABEL KID.*

how his old commanding officer had fared and what had become of him after the French's defeat and flight from Mexico. Apparently he had come through safely and had made some useful, lucrative contacts.

'While I have a good reason for becoming Colonel Anton de Richelieu,' the man continued. 'I am puzzled why you should claim to be Captain Fog.'

'I've my reasons,' Mark admitted and edged around until he could see Corbeau as well as keeping the other men covered.

'What reasons?' demanded the Creole indignantly, his face working angrily and fingers going closer to the Webley's butt.

'Private ones,' Mark replied. Almost casually, his left-hand Colt swung its muzzle to point at Corbeau's chest. 'Don't try it, major. *I'm* not expecting *you* to side me against anybody.'

'That's no answer,' growled one of the men at the table; before Corbeau could comment, although he showed that he understood Mark's meaning.

'It's all the answer I aim to give, asked this way,' the blond declared.

'The odds are against you,' warned the captain who was kneeling alongside Roxby's body. 'We could enforce our demands for an answer.'

'You could *try*,' Mark drawled, making a slight gesture with his Colt. 'But the Brotherhood will be shy at least two of its officers before I go under.'

'You've not changed, Mr. Counter,' de Richelieu commented and his voice seemed to hint at approval. 'Will you tell me your reasons, in private?'

There was only one reply that Mark could give. 'Yes, sir. I'll tell you, in private.'

'You won't need your guns. So put them up and come with me.'

'Roxby's dead and Brown soon will be,' the kneeling captain remarked.

'I'll accept that you had good reasons for killing them, Mr. Counter,' de Richelieu told Mark.

'May I go on record as saying that they drew first on

Capt—Mr. Counter, sir?' a third officer inquired, darting an accusative glance at Corbeau. 'Even if their deaths have deprived us of the services of two useful men.'

'Useful!' Corbeau spat back. 'Cheap hireling killers——.'

'Who were, at least, what they pretended to be,' the third officer, a surly-featured, paunchy major, pointed out.

'And what does that mean, Kincaid?' Corbeau demanded hotly.

'Gentlemen!' de Richelieu snapped, bringing both men's eyes in his direction. 'If you have nothing better to do than stand bickering, I would suggest that you take yourselves to bed.'

'Brown's gone,' remarked the captain who had been examining the stricken men. 'I'll fetch a detail and have them removed.'

'Perhaps you'll attend to that, Major Kincaid?' de Richelieu ordered, for the officer and Corbeau were still glaring at each other. 'Major Corbeau. Would you be good enough to go to the camp and inform the sergeant of the guard that there is no reason for him to come and investigate the shooting?'

'Yo!' Corbeau assented and stamped from the room.

'Come with me, Mr. Counter,' de Richelieu commanded and walked back into the room from which he had emerged.

Following his old commanding officer, Mark found himself in a small, snug den. De Richelieu waved him into the chair at the front of the desk and took a seat on the other side.

'It's been a long time, Maj—Colonel,' Mark commented, declining the offer of a cigar.

'I wouldn't come back until I was in a position to help the South,' de Richelieu answered. 'But I'm interested to hear why you claimed to be Captain Fog.'

At that moment, footsteps pattered in the hall. Lighter steps than would have been made by male footwear, they came to a halt outside the den. Its second door opened and a tall, shapely, beautiful woman walked in. Taken with the long white robe she wore, the pumps on her feet and her somewhat disheveled shortish auburn hair suggested that she had only recently left her bed.

'I heard shots, Anton,' the woman stated in a deep, husky contralto voice. Cold, appraising eyes flickered to Mark as he, like de Richelieu, came to his feet. 'So *this* is the famous Captain Fog?'

'No, Virginie,' de Richelieu contradicted. 'This is not Captain Fog.'

'Did Corbeau's men have to kill him?' the woman asked brutally.

'It was all a misunderstanding,' de Richelieu replied, scowling. 'Mr. Counter, may I present the Baroness de Vautour. Baroness, this is Mr. Counter, he was a first lieutenant under my command. Corbeau mistook him for Captain Fog.'

'Mr. Counter,' the woman greeted, advancing and extending her right hand. Her grip was strong, cool and impersonal as she shook hands.

'Ma'am,' the big blond acknowledged.

'Please be seated, gentlemen,' Virginie commanded regally and, after they had obeyed, went on, 'Which of those fools was it this time?'

'Mr. Counter——' de Richelieu began.

'Not another noble exponent of the *code duello*, surely,' Virginie interrupted, eyeing the blond giant with cold, barely hidden contempt.

'I don't go around looking for reasons to slap another feller's face and call him to meet me at dawn,' Mark told her calmly. 'But, happens somebody concludes to shoot me, I figure I've a right to stop him.'

'I suppose Roxby and Brown had some grudge against you, Mr. Counter?' de Richelieu asked.

'*They* figured they had,' Mark drawled and told why the pair had hated him.

'What a remarkable judge of character Major Kincaid is,' Virginie purred. 'But where is Captain Fog? Corbeau's message said——.'

'That Captain Fog was in town and he intended to

either get "me" to join the Brotherhood, or have me killed in a way that would rile up the townsfolk against the Yankees.'

'A shrewd assumption, Mr. Counter,' Virginie praised, eyeing him with added interest.

'It cost you two more *good* men,' Mark warned. 'Corbeau and Petain killed the "soldiers".'

'They were expendable,' Virginie answered, clearly dismissing Jan and the corporal as of no importance.

'A pair of drunken, sullen malcontents, who were spreading ill-feeling amongst our soldiers,' de Richelieu elaborated.

'So you sent them in to Los Cabestrillo to get them killed,' Mark guessed. 'To have them make a fuss with the folks and wind up wolf-bait. Only Corbeau saw a better way of using them.'

'That doesn't tell us why you pretended to be Captain Fog,' Virginie put in, before de Richelieu could confirm or deny the blond giant's comment.

Something about the woman's attitude annoyed Mark. So he decided that he would try to ruin her cool, slightly mocking and detached poise.

'I never said that I'd tell *us*",' the blond said to de Richelieu. 'What I have to say is private, Colonel.'

Mark had achieved his end. Letting out an angry cluck, Virginie went to the third chair and sat deliberately on it.

Since her arrival, the big Texan had been studying Virginie with considerable interest. Beautiful, beyond any question, she had a·magnificent, full-bosomed, slender-waisted figure which the flimsy robe emphasized to its best. If her title was genuine, she must have married a foreigner. Her accent was American, well-educated and Northern in its origin. There was an air of standing no nonsense about her and more than a hint of temper in the set of her full lips.

However, Baroness or plain Mrs., if she wanted a clash of wills, Mark was willing to accommodate her.

Not only that. The blond giant could see that his next actions might be of tremendous importance.

From the start, Mark had known that General Hardin would not support a movement that might once again plunge the United States into the bloody hell of a civil war. In fact, loyal as he undoubtedly was to the South, Ole Devil would take steps to have such an attempt suppressed. To do so would require information concerning the people involved and the means by which they hoped to achieve their ends.

If the Brotherhood For Southron Freedom had been comprised solely of men like Corbeau, Petain and the 'soldiers', Mark would have dismissed them as all puff, blow and bellow; nothing more than a noisy nuisance. With Byron Aspley—or *Colonel* Anton de Richelieu —in command, especially if the stories of his powerful European backing should be true, the organization was a horse of a very different, vastly more dangerous color.

Knowing that the question of his assumed identity could not be shelved and forgotten, the big blond had been wondering how he might best explain it. At first, he had considered saying that he was merely making the most of the benefits which accrued from being 'Captain Dusty Fog' instead of plain Mark Counter. It would be logical and easily understandable—but would not show his own character in a creditable light.

Far better, Mark concluded, to devise a stronger reason. One that would bring him favorably to the Baroness's and de Richelieu's attention. First, however, he had to put them in the correct frame of mind. Allowing himself to be browbeaten by a woman was not the way to do that.

'How have things been with you since Mexico, Colonel?' Mark inquired, in the manner of making idle conversation, and hooked his right foot up onto his left knee.

'The Baroness has my full confidence, Mr. Counter,' de Richelieu growled; but the big Texan sensed that he was not entirely opposed to the way things were going.

'That doesn't mean she has mine,' Mark pointed out

and felt sure that he saw a flicker of approval on the other man's lean face.

'Suppose that *we* insist upon you answering, Mr. Counter?' Virginie challenged, studying his giant frame with cold eyes.

'Roxby and Brown're good reasons for *you* not to have it *tried*, ma'am,' the Texan answered.

'You might not find others of our men so easy to handle,' Virginie warned.

'Maybe not, ma'am,' Mark drawled, knowing instinctively that he was handling her in the best possible manner. 'But it'll cost you a few more of them, trying to show me how good they are.'

'He's speaking the truth, Virginie,' de Richelieu put in quietly. 'Unless he's lost his ability—and the two men suggest that he hasn't—we don't have a man who is his equal with a revolver.'

The Baroness did not answer for several seconds. Flickering her gaze from one man to the other, she seemed to be trying to bring them under the influence of her will. At last she conceded that she could not and gave a shrug.

'Then we'd be advised to let him tell us in his own way,' Virginie said and made as if to rise.

'I'd be honored if you'd stay and listen, ma'am,' Mark declared, having made his point and certain that such permission would further suit his needs. He carried on as if satisfied that his offer would be accepted. 'Tempers are a mite high over that Army beef contract. Shanghai Pierce and the others figure that, us having helped the Yankees a few times since the War——'

'You have,' Virginie agreed thoughtfully.

'We'd good enough reasons, ma'am. Anyways, Shanghai's bunch figured Ole Devil's got enough pull to swing the contract our way no matter what they say. So they're not fixing to do any saying.'

'I don't follow you,' de Richelieu stated.

'They reckon that, happen the OD Connected doesn't send a representative to that old meeting, the Army will have to find against us.'

'So Captain Fog has kept you back from that shipment and is using you as a lure to draw Pierce and the others off the track.'

'Yes, ma'am. Only I was never onto the ship. That was to keep them from figuring there's too many "Dusty Fogs" around and about.'

'And where is Captain Fog now?' de Richelieu demanded.

'Back home on the spread,' Mark lied. 'We don't want it running over with hired guns. So I've been roaming around, telling folks I'm Dusty and hoping to draw off any who've been hired.'

'Don't you mind being used that way?' Virginie asked, frowning.

'Shucks, no,' the blond giant grinned. 'It beats plain old working on the spread. And folks're sure accommodating to "Captain Dusty Fog". More than they'd be to plain ole "Mark Counter".'

Watching an exchange of glances between Virginie and de Richelieu, Mark guessed that his story had been accepted and that he had achieved his intention. They were impressed by his loyalty to the OD Connected and his casual acceptance of a dangerous assignment.

'Why did General Hardin send Captain Fog to Sheldon?' de Richelieu inquired.

'Because he figured that our men could do more for the South back home,' Mark answered. 'And he was satisfied that we'd get better treatment from the Yankees for coming back when *they* wanted us to.'

'Shrewd thinking,' Virginie praised.

'He's a mighty shrewd man, ma'am,' Mark replied. 'He saw early that the only way of getting Texas over the effects of losing the War was to play along with the Yankees.'

'How do *you* feel about it?' de Richelieu challenged.

'Things were bad, Colonel. I figured we should take any means to make them better. And, down in Mexico, it wouldn't have been long before our men had insisted on coming home. They didn't like the French in any shape or form.'

Watching the couple, Mark discovered that the woman did not appear to be annoyed at the remark. Possibly her marriage had not given her any respect, love or pride in France.

'It's a pity you aren't Captain Fog,' Virginie remarked. 'We could do with a man like him here.'

'How's that, ma'am?' Mark inquired.

'You've seen Corbeau, Kincaid and the others?' Virginie answered.

'Yes'm.'

'What do you think of them?'

'I haven't known them long enough——'

'Which means that you think as I do,' the woman guessed. 'That not one of them is worth a damn as an officer.'

'Corbeau's a good administrator,' de Richelieu put in.

'When we need one, he'll be a blessing,' Virginie answered. 'The others are all right in their fields—but their fields aren't much use to us right now.'

'Why's that, ma'am?' Mark wanted to know.

'Because not one of them has the qualities it takes to weld a bunch of men into a fighting regiment,' the Baroness explained. 'Especially when they don't have the weight of a formal Army's disciplinary machine behind them.'

'How about Petain?' Mark asked.

'An arrogant bully, with a mean, vicious streak,' Virginie stated. 'He would make a fine commandant for a penal colony, or chief torturer for a medieval court.'

'He isn't a leader,' de Richelieu agreed. 'And it's a leader I need to whip my men into shape.'

'You could do it, Colonel,' Mark said and was sincere.

'Thank you,' de Richelieu answered. 'But I have other things to do. What we need, if all I've heard of him is true, is a man like Captain Fog.'

'As Anton says,' Virginie went on, eyeing Mark in an appraising manner. 'A man *like* Captain Fog.'

''So you've got "Captain Fog" here right now,' the

big blond drawled, grabbing his chance in both hands.

'You mean——?' the Baroness prompted.

'Have you many Texas boys around?' Mark asked.

'None. Anton sent men from east of the Mississippi out here. It was easier in the South to select those we could be reasonably sure of trusting.'

'Being the kind of outfit we are, we thought it advisable on another score,' de Richelieu took up where the woman had finished. 'Even in the Army, Texans were notorious for not being amenable to discipline when it was applied by what they chose to regard as dudes.'

'I saw some of it,' Mark admitted with a grin. 'Are there any of them likely to know Dusty?'

'It's not likely,' de Richelieu claimed.

'Then, providing your officers haven't been flapping their lips too much about what's gone on,' Mark drawled, 'you-all can do like I've been doing—and getting away with. Pass me off as Dusty Fog.'

'It could work, Anton!' Virginie ejaculated.

'It could,' de Richelieu agreed. 'Mr. Counter was a promising young officer and I wouldn't be surprised if he hasn't learned some of Captain Fog's tricks. If only they haven't blabbed—— I'll go and see. Virginie, just in case we need them, could you go and wake up Pieber and his assistant?'

'Who are they?' Mark asked.

'Our tailors,' Virginie answered. 'By morning, I want to see you in a Cavalry captain's uniform.'

CHAPTER TEN

You Tried to Get Me Killed

'This is the best we could do in the time, Captain Fog,' apologized the plump, red-faced Albert Pieber—in the mock deprecatory tone of one who knew that he had done an excellent piece of work—as he watched the blond giant draw on the tunic which he had made during what remained of the night.

'Happen it fits as comfortable as the breeches,' Mark Counter answered, 'it'll be real fine.'

Having accepted the idea that they might be able to pass off Mark as Dusty Fog, Baroness Virginie and de Richelieu had wasted no time in implementing the scheme. De Richelieu's questioning had satisfied him that his 'officers' had not told the 'enlisted men' of Corbeau's mistake. Probably the Creole had had something to do with their reticence, for he had been furious over his error and in a dangerous mood. Or their silence may have stemmed from another source. Being aware of how slender a hold they had over the lower ranks of the Brotherhood, they had hesitated to let it become known that two of the 'officers' had been hoodwinked.

So excellent had the web of secrecy been that even Petain did not know of Mark's true identity. Inadvertently, the young Creole had helped to divert the 'enlisted men's' interest from the shooting of Roxby and Brown. As Mark and Corbeau had suspected, the young man had gone in search of the vedette who had neglected to challenge them on their arrival. After a

97

search, Petain had located the man asleep under a tree. Going up quietly, he had taken the vedette's rifle. Kicking the man awake, he had smashed the butt of the rifle onto his head as he rose still half-asleep. Then, leaving his victim sprawled on the ground with a fractured skull, Petain had gone to send the sergeant of the guard to collect him. The Creole's action had been sufficient to lessen the speculation that might have otherwise been felt over the two men's deaths.

On returning to the main house, full of his importance and efficiency, Petain had not been pleased to hear that 'Captain Fog' was to assume command of the training schedule. However, the Creole had kept his thoughts to himself and stalked angrily off to his room.

For his part, Mark had spent a most useful and instructive couple of hours before going to the quarters which were assigned to him. He had seen something of the extent to which the Brotherhood's preparations had advanced. Even if he had doubted it before, he had then realized just how serious a threat they might easily become.

Not only had de Richelieu been able to produce sufficient cadet-gray cloth, brass buttons, gold braid and other items to create a uniform, he had also located a weapon belt and a pair of Hessian boots for Mark to wear. Pieber and his assistant, fetched from their quarters by the Baroness, had taken their measurements and worked without stopping until they had delivered the first outfit.

So Mark had found himself donning the yellow-striped breeches of a Cavalryman once more. Like the breeches, the tunic proved to be an excellent fit. It had a formal stand-up collar, although bearing a captain's three gold bars and not the two of a first lieutenant. The sleeves, with the two strands of gold braid twisted into the 'chicken-guts' Austrian knots on each of them, and the double-breasted front, bearing two rows of seven brass buttons, were of formal, correct pattern. There was, however, one innovation which Mark had insisted

upon. He had caused the tunic's skirt 'extending half-
way between his hip and knee', as the *Manual of Dress
Regulations* prescribed, to be omitted.

Although it had been Mark himself who had first
done this—incurring the displeasure of numerous hide-
bound senior officers—he had explained that Dusty Fog
was one of the many young Southern bloods who had
followed his lead in flouting the Regulations.

On another matter Mark had been equally adamant.
Again he was helped by well-known facts. The Texas
Light Cavalry had been noted for wearing western-style
gunbelts. So Mark could continue to use his *buscadero*
rig without losing credibility.

That had been a relief to the blond giant. Knowing
the desperate nature of the men with whom he was
dealing, he wanted his weapons to be a damned sight
more easily available than in a close-topped, high
riding, twist-hand draw holster.

'We have made you a cravat, sir,' Pieber hinted, as
Mark left the collar open sufficiently for him to fasten
on his bandana.

'I only wear one in full dress,' the blond answered,
secure in the knowledge that it was another detail he and
Dusty had had in common. 'You've done a real fine
job, *monsieur*.'

'*Danke schön!*' the tailor answered; his pleasure at
the praise was tinged with annoyance and irritation for
some reason.

Mark was not given the opportunity to ponder on the
man's contradictory attitudes. At that moment there
was a knock at the room's door. It was not the sound of
a person giving notice of wishing to come in, but a
demand to enter.

'Who is it?' Mark called.

'Baroness de Vautour,' came back the answer in
Virginie's voice. 'May I come in?'

The polite words sounded more like, 'Open the door,
I insist on coming in.'

Darting an apologetic glance at the blond giant, but

without permitting him to make known his sentiments on the matter, Pieber scuttled hurriedly to the door. The tailor jerked it open. Then he and his assistant slammed into rigid postures of attention. Watching them, Mark could not remember ever having seen Maximilian's French troops display such a high standard of military smartness.

Wearing a neat, plain, figure-concealing, yet expensive gray serge two-piece traveling costume, the Baroness swept regally into the room. She had taken her hair back tightly, concealing it under a gray Baden hat that resembled a narrow-brimmed, low-crowned Stetson which had been decorated with a wide black lace band and a cluster of white ibis feathers.

Clearly she did not consider the tailors as being of sufficient importance to warrant a glance. Advancing across the room in what—if it had been done by another women with her physical attributes—would have been a sensual glide, she contrived to look as if she was marching in a military review.

'Good morning, Mis——,' Virginie began, chopping off her words angrily as she realized what she had been on the point of saying.

'*Captain* Fog, ma'am,' Mark supplied, being unable to resist the temptation to try and break down her composure.

'Good morning, *Captain* Fog!' Virginie spat out viciously, cheeks reddening.

Holding her temper with an effort, the Baroness stalked around the big blond. She studied him with the air of a rancher examining an animal before deciding to purchase it. Off to one side, still rigidly at attention, the tailors displayed a wooden apprehension as they watched her making the inspection.

'I hope it meets with your approval, ma'am,' Mark drawled, his whole attitude suggesting that he did not care a damn one way or the other about her opinion. Taking up his gunbelt, he buckled it on.

'It will do,' Virginie said off-handedly and the tailors beamed as if they had received a hearty vote of thanks for their efforts. 'Have you had breakfast?'

'Not yet,' Mark admitted.

'Then I would suggest that you do so. After you've finished, we'll take you to meet your troops.'

'I was just going to say that's what I aimed to do.'

Sucking in a deep breath, Virginie spun on her heels and almost stamped her way across the room towards the door. The Texan's hateful voice followed her.

'I'd already thanked these gentlemen for doing such good work. But I reckon they're pleased that *you* approve.'

Pieber had bounded to the door and jerked it open, without appearing to have lost his rigid brace. There was an expression of awe on his face as he watched Mark stroll out after the Baroness. Clearly the tailor had never expected to see anybody treat her with other than slavish, abject respect.

'You'll try my patience once too often, *Mister* Counter!' Virginie hissed furiously as she and the big Texan started to descend to the ground floor.

'Just so *you* don't try *mine* too far, Baroness,' Mark answered, with no display of alarm over the threat. 'And the name is *Captain Dustine Edward Marsden Fog*. Remember?'

If looks could have killed, Mark Counter would not have lived long enough to become the great-grandfather of a jet-age peace officer who would handle a handgun with as much skill as shown by any of the legendary Old West *pistoleros*.*

Having tried, and failed, to quell the Texan with a cold, icy glare, Virginie almost ran down the stairs. In the hall, she led the way to the dining-room which faced the study. Going in, Mark found all but Petain of the officers present. The blond was conscious of the other men's scrutiny and wondered how many of them would have bitterly opposed his wearing the skirtless tunic if he had been under their command during the War.

* Mark Counter's great-grandson, Bradford, appears in the author's Rockabye County stories.

'Good morning, sir, gentlemen,' Mark greeted formally as he went to the table.

A Mexican waiter drew out a chair for the Baroness and another prepared a place for Mark.

'Are you staying with us for long this time, Baroness?' Corbeau inquired.

'No,' Virginie replied. 'I want to make sure things are ready in Austin for the magician's arrival.'

'Sabot won't be going to Austin,' de Richelieu remarked and something in his voice brought immediate silence to the men and woman around the table. Their attention went to him. 'When you've finished breakfast, Captain Fog, I want you to accompany the Baroness and myself to the camp.'

'Yo!' Mark affirmed.

'The rest of you gentlemen have your duties,' de Richelieu went on, his manner indicating that the subject was closed.

'Talking of duties,' Kincaid remarked. 'Young Petain's starting to take his real seriously. Here it is not yet ten o'clock and he's up and gone to the camp.'

'Maybe he's gone to apologize to the man whose head he busted,' Captain Raphael—the man who had examined Mark's victims—commented. 'That was a damned stupid thing to do. We're not an Army—yet.'

The last word had clearly come as an afterthought, brought about by the cold glare which de Richelieu had directed at the speaker. Lowering his gaze to his plate, Raphael went on with his breakfast.

Half an hour later, Mark rode with Virginie and de Richelieu towards the Brotherhood's camp. It was set up in a wide, but well-sheltered and hidden valley. Again the blond giant was impressed by the standard of the equipment. Even from the rim, he could see that the rows of Sibley, 'umbrella', wall and wedge tents were new and in excellent condition. Horses stood along picket lines at the far side of the valley. Down at the foot of the slope, ahead of Mark's party, Petain stood watching over a hundred men in cadet-gray cavalry

uniforms forming—ambling and slouching being more
descriptive—into three slovenly, crooked ranks.

'You see what we're up against, Mr. Counter?' de
Richelieu demanded, reining his mount to a stop and indicating the assembled men. 'They're still no better than
a disorganized rabble.'

'Looks that way,' Mark conceded.

'I was in Europe in '70 and '71,' de Richelieu continued. 'And I saw what happened to badly, or wrongly,
disciplined troops.'

'That was when the French and Prussians were
fussing, huh?'

'Yes. The French had their *Chassepot* breech-loading
rifles and the new *Mitrailleuse* machine guns that are a
vast improvement over the Gatling, against the Prussians' needle-guns. Yet they were still defeated.
Discipline is what brought it about, Mr. Counter. The
Prussians had it. The French didn't.'

'That's true,' Virginie confirmed, concealing any bitterness she might have felt over her husband's country
having met a crushing defeat.

'I'll see if I can lick 'em into shape,' Mark promised.
' 'Least, I know how Dusty would go about it; and I
reckon his way's good enough for me. Let's go and
make a stab at it.' As the horses started moving, he went
on, 'Who-all's the worst trouble-maker?'

'Cyrus Purge——,' de Richelieu began without
hesitation.

'The same Cyrus Purge who took that Yankee
Napoleon single-handed at Spotsylania, then turned it
on the other guns in the battery?'

'The very same,' de Richelieu agreed.

'He's that big, dirty, hulking brute in the center of the
front rank,' Virginie elaborated.

'The rest follow him, huh, Colonel?' Mark drawled,
finding no difficulty in picking out the man in question.

Massively built, Cyrus Purge stood in the position
which Virginie had mentioned. He had his hands thrust
insolently into his pockets and was clearly enjoying

being the center of attention. Grinning men nudged each other in the ribs and nodded towards the approaching trio, then at Purge.

'He has a lot of influence,' de Richelieu admitted.

'Shoot the mutinous son-of-a-bitch!' Virginie advised savagely, jerking a contemptuous thumb towards the young Creole captain. 'Petain should have done it the first time Purge showed signs of disobedience. I'm surprised he didn't.'

'Maybe *he's* smart enough to know that doing it would lose the Brotherhood more than it would gain,' Mark drawled. 'The French were all for shooting fellers, but it didn't do them much good in Mexico. Nor against the Prussians, way the Colonel tells it.' Ignoring the glare of hatred the Baroness threw at him, he continued, 'Reckon he'd make a good man, Colonel?'

'He *could* be a power of good, if he'd take discipline,' de Richelieu declared. 'But, so far, I've not had a man capable of winning his respect and making him accept it.'

'But Mr. Counter thinks he can!' Virginie spat out.

'If you can't remember I'm "Captain Fog", ma'am,' Mark growled. 'I'd sooner say the hell with this whole idea. It won't work.'

'Remember what I said to you earlier this morning, *Captain Fog!*' Virginie hissed, her right hand tightening on the grip of the heavy quirt she carried until the knuckles showed pallid white through the tight-stretched skin.

'And you keep on minding the answer, ma'am,' Mark warned. 'Anybody who tried to lay a quirt on me—Well, I might not let whoever *tried* being a woman stop me stopping them.'

'Anton!' Virginie shrilled, but let the quirt drop to dangle by its wrist strap. 'Are you going to allow——.'

'The Colonel knows I'm right about the name, ma'am,' Mark drawled. 'If somebody calls me the wrong name, it could blow the whole Brotherhood to pieces. Men don't take kindly to thinking somebody's been trying to hoodwink them.'

'*Captain Fog* is right about that,' de Richelieu confirmed, laying great emphasis on the first two words. 'We mustn't make mistakes. There's too much at stake for that.'

'On the other thing, ma'am,' Mark went on. 'The Colonel likely thinks it's a personal matter between you and me.'

By that time, they had reached the foot of the slope. Still the 'soldiers' made little more than a token attempt to form their ranks. Watching them, Mark sensed an air of expectancy in the way their eyes remained upon him. He knew instinctively that it was connected in some way with the big, heavily built Purge.

Urging his mount forward at a slightly faster pace, Mark swung from its saddle in front of Purge's position in the ranks. He allowed the split-end reins to drop from his fingers, 'ground hitching' the animal as effectively as if it had been tied to a snubbing post. Then he strolled, smartly yet nonchalantly, towards the 'soldiers'. Behind him, Virginie and de Richelieu halted their horses. They remained in their saddles, watching his every move.

'This is Captain Fog,' Petain commented, throwing a meaningful glance at Purge.

'He the feller you-all allows is going to make us toe the line like we'n's's regular Army?' Purge inquired.

A dull red flush crept over the Creole's handsome features. It was clear that the comment had displeased him. However, Mark gave no sign of having understood the enormous man's meaning.

'If I didn't see the uniforms,' Mark said to Petain, making sure that his words could be heard by the assembled men but never as much as glancing in Purge's direction, 'I'd swear they were *Yankees*. Don't you see to it that they wash, shave and tidy themselves up for Colonel's muster, Captain Petain?'

'I thought I'd leave that to you!' the Creole gritted, almost quivering with rage at the rebuke.

'I'm right pleased you did,' Mark declared, advancing but avoiding any obvious scrutiny of Purge. In fact, he seemed to be looking everywhere except at the brawny man. 'You damned, hawg-filthy——.'

Conscious that every 'soldier's' eyes were on him, Purge decided that he must assert himself. He equaled the blond giant in height and, with his barrel-like belly, was far heavier. Long brown hair covered his ears and caused the kepi to perch like a bump on a log. Blowing out his cheeks, he started to step from the ranks.

'Can't say's I take kind——!' Purge began.

He advanced only one pace.

Like a flash, Mark pivoted at the hips and threw the full power of his two-hundred-and-eighteen-pound frame behind a back-hand slap to the side of Purge's head. Taken by surprise, with his right leg in the air for his second step, the burly man was twirled around. He lost his kepi as he blundered into and brought down four other men with the force of the collision. Yells and curses rose on all sides.

Down flipped Mark's right hand, joining the left as it swept the nearside Peacemaker from leather. Both guns lifted, swinging their muzzles in an arc which encompassed the men who had been closest to Purge and who were, Mark assumed, his special cronies.

Sitting up and rubbing the back of his right hand against his right cheek, Purge shook his head. Then he lurched erect and glared at the blond Texan beyond the two Peacemakers.

'Now that's a whole heap of dee-fense, even for an officer ag'in an 'listed man,' Purge growled.

'If those things are worrying you,' Mark drawled, gesturing with the Colts. 'I'll have Captain Petain hold 'em.'

With that, the big blond lowered the hammers and tossed the revolvers to the Creole.

Immediately, letting out a whoop, Purge charged forward. He believed that he was going to take Mark as unawares as he had been. Always a plain roughhouse brawler, willing to take all his opponent could give and confident that he could more than repay it, the soldier expected Mark to duplicate his style of fighting.

That was where Purge made another mistake. Mark had learned the art of self-defense from a man who had known the value of protective methods. So he knew just how to deal with a blind, bull-like charge.

Side-stepping Purge's clumsy rush, Mark hurled his left hand into the pit of the other's belly. The impact halted the huge man, causing him to feel that the rock-hard fist was shoving his guts into his backbone. Watching Purge fold over, the blond giant stepped behind him. Up swung Mark's right boot, laying its sole on the man's pants' seat and pushing. Sent forward, Purge lit down on his face almost at Petain's feet.

Acting as if startled, the Creole jumped away and dropped Mark's Colts in front of Purge. Gasping for breath, the big soldier hunched himself onto his knees. Scrabbling for support, his right hand came to rest on the butt of Mark's lefthand Colt. Before Purge's mind could take in what the thing under his palm might be, Mark was already moving towards him. Bending, the Texan hooked both hands into Purge's tunic's collar. Then Mark exerted all his enormous strength in a lifting heave. Purge rose from the ground like a pheasant rocketing out of cover. Witnesses later claimed that his feet were elevated some six inches above the grass. Hurled away by his captor, Purge went spinning and teetering. This time the crowd scattered hurriedly in all directions and he did not have other bodies to cushion his fall.

Silence fell over the soldiers and they stared in awe from Purge to the big Texan who had handled him with such ease. Slowly, painfully, Purge eased himself into a sitting position. Once more he shook his head. Admiration showed on his face as he saw the blond looming menacingly in his direction.

'You feel that strong about it, Cap'n Fog,' Purge said, grinning amiably. 'I'll go 'n' wash 'n' shave right now.'

'You do that,' Mark agreed, offering his hand and helping Purge rise. 'And the rest of you hear this. In one hour, I'm coming to make inspection. By then, I'll ex-

pect to see you looking like soldiers of the Confederate
States Army. Dismiss!'

Watching the hurried disintegration of the crowd, the
big blond knew that he had achieved one thing. He
would now have no trouble in controlling the men.
There was, however, another matter to take up. Returning, he picked up and holstered his Colts. Then he
strode over and confronted the Creole.

'You lousy Cree-owl pelican!' Mark growled. 'You
tried to get me killed.'

'I don't know what——,' Petain began, throwing a
look to where Virginie and de Richelieu had started to
ride forward.

'You dropped my guns purposely, so that Purge
would pick one up and turn it on me,' Mark elaborated.
'That way, you'd be rid of both of us. The Colonel
would have had him shot for doing it.'

'I won't even trouble to deny it,' Petain declared
haughtily. 'My seconds will call on you.'

With that, the Creole turned and stalked away. He
went at such an angle that his right side and hand were
hidden from Mark's view. Carefully, he eased out the
Army Colt from its twist-draw holster. With the weapon
in his hand, he swung fully sideways on and began to
elevate the weapon to shoulder height.

In the process of adopting his duelist's stance, Petain
learned the basic and very deadly difference between his
style of fighting and that of his proposed victim.

Looking along the barrel to align his sights, he
watched the blond giant crouch slightly. Mark's hands
whipped hipwards. Before Petain's brain could
assimilate what was happening, he saw the two
Peacemakers appear from their holsters and point his
way. Flame and smoke gushed from their muzzles.

That was the last living memory of Paul Petain.

Passing under the Creole's raised right arm, two .45
bullets crashed between his ribs and tore his heart to
pieces. He was snapped backwards, firing a shot in-
voluntarily. Its bullet went into the air and he was dead
before his body struck the ground.

CHAPTER ELEVEN

Get Into My Bed

'May I come in, Captain Fog?' Virginie de Vautour asked, as Mark opened the door of his room to her knock.

It was night and the woman stood in the lamplight, dressed as she had been when he had first seen her; except that her hair was tidy. In her right hand, she grasped the neck of a wine bottle and her left fingers held the stems of two glasses. The robe hung open, exposing a diaphonous nightdress which made her look more naked than she would have been if she had been completely unclothed.

'I'm not dressed for having callers,' the big blond warned.

Which was true enough. Having been undressed ready to go to bed, Mark was wearing only his riding breeches. He had not recognized Virginie's knock, for it had a less commanding sound, and so he had opened up without troubling to don other garments.

After killing Petain, Mark had spent a very busy day.

Virginie and de Richelieu had stated that they could hardly blame Mark for defending himself, even to the extent of shooting the Creole. On hearing of the incident, the other officers had failed to display concern over Petain's death. All had seemed relieved, at least, to know that the hot-tempered, always quarrelsome Petain would no longer be around looking for ways to issue a challenge to a duel.

Giving the men the hour he had promised, and not a

second longer, Mark had had 'Assembly' blown by the
bugler. While they were still far from being perfect, the
improvement in their appearance and decorum had been
very marked. So much so that de Richelieu had stated
his satisfaction.

At the same time, de Richelieu had also explained
why there were no men from Sheldon's Regiment
amongst the Brotherhood. Recalling with deep bitterness how they had accepted Grant's offer to return to
their homes, he had been disinclined to turn to his old
comrades-in-arms for support. Having now seen how
effective one of them could be, he was contemplating
changing his mind. Wishing to avoid bringing men who
had been his friends into the affair, Mark had pointed
out that doing so would increase the danger of
somebody letting slip his true identity.

Mark had given the men little rest all that day.
Pushing them hard, he had caused the tent lines to be
straightened, the area policed until there was not so
much as a cigarette butt in the living area or the horse
lines. There had been a longer grooming session than
any of the animals had ever suffered before,
examinations of their condition and exercise periods.
Weapons had had to be produced and put through a
rigorous scrutiny. Finally, Mark had made certain that
the members of the Brotherhood would have plenty to
occupy their time until 'lights out' was blown.

Mark had been pleased with his work. While he was
welding the Brotherhood into an efficient fighting unit,
he had felt sure that the majority of them would soon
give him their loyalty. There was, however, a hard core
of Secessionist fanatics who would remain true to de
Richelieu. They—most of them were non-commissioned
officers—were the real danger and had, in Mark's
opinion, a far greater potential than Corbeau or the
other 'officers'.

Stepping in as the big blond withdrew, Virginie
kicked the door closed with her heel. Then she held out
the bottle and glasses.

'Was I a suspicious sort of feller,' Mark drawled,

without taking them. 'I'd be wondering why you've come.'

'How do you mean?' the Baroness inquired.

'Seems like every time we've met today, I've raked you with my spurs.'

'Or I've raked you,' Virginie pointed out. 'So I think it's time we called a truce, don't you?'

'Why the change of heart?'

'Why do you think?'

'Lady, I don't know—but I aim to find out.'

'I consider that you are the best man here,' Virginie assured him, still holding her smile even if it ended clear of her eyes. There was something cold and wary in them. 'None of the others, even de Richelieu, could have done what you accomplished today. So I've decided that we must end our differences.'

'How'd your husband feel about that, ma'am?' Mark asked.

'He's dead.'

'Do I say I'm sorry?'

'It's a matter of indifference. Raoul and I weren't the same age and had little in common. For one thing, he chose the wrong side in the Franco-Prussian War. That was a fatal choice for a man with all his estates and assets tied up in the Alsace. Well, do we drink and become friends?'

'I'm all for friendship,' Mark declared and relieved her of her burdens.

'Do you have to drink—*first*?' Virginie purred as Mark stood at the side-piece pouring wine into the glasses.

Looking around, Mark found that the Baroness had slipped off her robe. It lay on the floor and she was walking toward him. He set down the bottle and glass, swinging to face her. The nightdress had a slit from hem almost to its waist. As she advanced, first one, then the other shapely leg came into view.

The big blond concluded that she did not really need *that* effect.

Reaching out, Mark prepared to scoop her into his

arms. For all that, he could not shake off an uneasy feeling that all was far from being well. He had had a fair amount of experience with women and success in attracting them. Without being unduly immodest, he was aware that he had physical attributes which the opposite sex found most attractive. Accepting that a woman might take such steps to improve their relationship, he was still puzzled at why that particular one would do so. It was, he felt, completely out of character for Virginie de Vautour to come—cap-in-hand, as it were—to beg forgiveness from a man who had repeatedly antagonized her.

With that in mind, while willing to accept the olive branch Virginie had offered, Mark wondered what had caused her to come to his room.

He learned the reason quickly enough!

Even as he touched the warm, smooth flesh of her shoulders, an alarm bell triggered off a warning in his mind. Her skin felt warm, yet he could sense that tension and not eager response lay beneath it. Added to that, he saw all the seductive expression leave her face. It was replaced by a glow of growing triumph. Instead of a potential lover, Virginie resembled a poker-playing bull about to bring off a master-stroke that would completely defeat an opponent.

Up hurled the Baroness's left leg, aiming its knee towards Mark's groin. It failed to reach its target, but not by any great margin. Alert for the possibility of treachery, the blond giant had turned the pull which would have brought her up close into a punch. At the same instant, he swiveled his body away. Instead of impacting against the ultra-sensitive region, her knee caught him on the thigh. It arrived hard enough to warn him of what would have happened had it reached its intended target.

'You bitch!' Mark growled, thrusting her from him.

'You bastard!' Virginie shrilled, catching her balance, coming to a halt and returning to throw a punch at the Texan's head.

Rising swiftly, Mark's right hand intercepted the

blow in mid-flight. His fingers closed around her wrist, grasping it savagely. Retreating, towing her after him effortlessly, he sat on the bed. While she must have known what he was intending, she could not prevent it happening. A quick jerk hauled her belly-down across his knees.

'This's what somebody should've done to you a long time ago!' Mark gritted.

Up and down rose his left hand, while the right transferred itself to the back of her neck and held her as helpless as a butterfly pinned to a collector's display card. His flat palm descended hard on her barely protected rump. Slap after slap rang out, while she struggled futilely, squealed in pain or yelped out curses in English and French.

After administering the spanking—which would have gladdened the hearts of numerous people, including the late Baron de Vautour, if they had been privileged to witness it—Mark rolled the woman from his knees. Turning over twice on the floor, Virginie landed supine. Tears streamed down her face as she sat up. Glaring at the big Texan, she was stopped from speaking by a realization that *sitting* was painful. So she rose, delicate fingers going to the fiery source of her discomfort and gently rubbing it.

'All right,' Mark drawled, standing up but not approaching her. 'Your little notion for showing me who's boss didn't work.'

'Wh—what are you going to do to me?' Virginie sniffed.

'That's up to you,' the blond replied. 'You can get into my bed, or you can get the hell back to your own room. Me, I'm going to finish undressing and put weight on the mattress.'

Turning and walking painfully, still rubbing at where her buttocks showed redder than the white of her skin under the nightdress, Virginie went to the door. Her fingers were on the knobs when she spun around.

'You big, handsome bastard!' the Baroness gasped and ran towards the blond giant.

This time there was no pretense, nor ulterior motive, in how she acted.

If any of the other men had heard the spanking, or otherwise been disturbed, they gave no hint of it at breakfast the following morning. Nor did the Baroness when she entered and gingerly took her seat at the table. The incident of the previous night might never have happened, but for a slight wince, which Mark alone observed, as she moved incautiously on her chair. She was still the same cool, distant, imperious Virginie de Vautour to everybody but the big blond. Him she ignored except for addressing the usual commonplaces.

'Will you come with the Baroness and me to my office, before you go to your duties, Captain Fog?' de Richelieu inquired as the meal ended.

'Yo!' Mark replied.

Having dismissed the others to their duties, de Richelieu escorted the woman and Mark into his small den. The Texan noted, without showing his amusement, that Virginie selected the softer of the guests' chairs and lowered herself onto it carefully.

'How will General Hardin react to our plans?' de Richelieu commenced, without preliminary formalities.

'He'll do whatever's best for the South,' Mark replied, evasively.

'And Captain Fog?'

'Him too.'

'Will they support us?' de Richelieu insisted.

'I wouldn't want to answer that "yes", or "no", in case I'm wrong,' Mark drawled. 'But I know they'll do the best for the South.'

'Which means they'll join us,' de Richelieu declared. 'Especially if——.'

'If——?' Virginie prompted.

'I would imagine that there will be considerable entertaining during the peace meeting with the ranchers, Mr. Counter?' de Richelieu said.

'You can count on it,' Mark agreed. 'Governor

Howard will want to keep everything friendly, and that's a right good way of doing it.'

'Including a visit to the theatre, if a suitable show was playing there,' Virginie said, her face showing understanding. 'What do you intend to do, Anton?'

'It's what Mr. Counter is going to do, my dear,' de Richelieu answered. ''He's going to persuade the Governor and the ranchers to attend a performance by Sabot the Mysterious——.'

'And?' the Baroness demanded eagerly.

'I haven't decided quite what we'll do yet,' de Richelieu admitted. 'But I've an idea that we can do what we planned to do in Shreveport. Only this time we'll make certain there are no mistakes.'

Although Mark hoped that he might gain a better idea of what de Richelieu was considering, the opportunity to do so was not presented. Instead, the leader of the Brotherhood came to his feet and intimated that the meeting was at an end. Politely, but in a manner which showed that he wanted no further discussion, he ushered Virginie and Mark from his den. In the hall, Virginie did not address a word to the blond giant, but strolled away in a preoccupied manner.

Collecting and saddling his horse, Mark rode to the camp. He too was preoccupied and deeply perturbed. Whatever de Richelieu was planning must be important, maybe even very dangerous for Dusty and the other ranchers. So Mark knew that he must discover what the scheme was going to be. The reference to Shreveport could possibly offer a clue.

Virginie had left the ranch when Mark returned that evening after putting his 'Company' through a grueling day they would be unlikely to forget for a long time. From what the blond was able to gather, the Baroness and Kincaid traveled from town to town—posing as man and wife—selecting potential supporters for the Cause. Having done so, they left written instructions—using a harmless-seeming but complex code—for use by the stage magician whom de Richelieu had mentioned. Apparently the Baroness and her 'husband' did not let themselves be known as part of the organization. It was Sabot the Mysterious who entertained the possible candidates, checked their loyalties, and spread the first seeds of the Brotherhood's propaganda.

In the days that followed Virginie's departure, Mark tried several times to gain some inkling of what de Richelieu was planning for the Governor's visit to San Antonio de Bexar. On each occasion the big blond had tried to raise the matter, the Colonel had grown evasive. De Richelieu merely stated that he had not yet formulated his plan, but when he did he would tell Mark everything.

Nor did the Texan have any greater luck in discovering what had happened in Shreveport. So well had Colonel Winslow done his work, that the story had not been printed in Texas newspapers. None of the men at the ranch appeared to know anything about the incident.

For his part, Mark went ahead with training the company. In that, he had practical experience as his guide and also the lessons in man-management which he had acquired from Dusty Fog. It was his intention to so sicken the men with their present life that they would desert and break away from the Brotherhood. So he drove them as hard as he could; which ought to have been a whole heap harder than they could take.

Each day, Mark held inspections of clothing, arms, equipment, horses, living accommodation. Not only that, but he filled their hours with drills, weapon training and a sequence of hard riding marches which reduced the participants to cursing, complaining masses of bruises.

To Mark, there were times when he felt that the clock had been turned back. He would ride at the head of his gray-clad company, with the Stars and Bars flag fluttering overhead, covering rough terrain at speed by the system known as 'posting the trot'.* That was a hard,

* Posting the trot is described in detail in: *UNDER THE STARS AND BARS.*

grueling and wearing method, until a man's muscles grew accustomed to it. However, any of the 'soldiers' who failed to do so found Mark at his side and roaring invective into his ears.

On the second day, three men 'deserted', but were caught by the fanatical non-coms. What happened to the trio caused all the others to reconsider if they had nourished plans of a similar nature.

Not only did the non-coms hold the men in check, Purge did more than his share. Filled with admiration for the blond giant who had defeated him, the burly man used his influence—which was still considerable—to keep others loyal to 'Captain Fog'.

The Baroness and her party returned, having left instructions for Sabot the Mysterious at Temple, in Bell County. When he received them, he would come to Los Cabestrillo and be delivered to the ranch. Virginie had called at the town on her return and brought Mark news from Marshal Flatter. Apparently the Kendal County sheriff had reached a decision concerning the deaths of the soldiers. No Army post admitted to having lost two of its men, so they were assumed to be deserters heading for the Mexican border. In which case, the sheriff considered that it would be sufficient if Captain Fog merely wrote and had witnessed a statement of what had happened.

Would Captain Fog go into Los Cabestrillo the following day and do it?

Accompanied by de Richelieu and Corbeau, all of them dressed in civilian clothing. Mark rode into the town shortly after noon on the appointed day. They were leaving their horses at the livery barn when Flatter arrived.

'Colonel!' the marshal said, mopping his face with a bandana.

'I thought I told you never to let on you knew me!' de Richelieu snarled.

'It's important!' Flatter protested. 'Them fellers who robbed the Yankee paymaster and killed all them blue-bellies——.'

'The Caxtons and Comanche Blood?' Corbeau put in.

'That's them!' Flatter agreed, delighted with the impression he was making on the three men.

'What about them?' de Richelieu demanded.

'They're up to the hotel now,' Flatter replied. 'In the dining-room, having a meal.'

'Are they?' de Richelieu said quietly. 'Come along, gentlemen. I'm looking forward to meeting them.'

CHAPTER TWELVE

Hands Flat on the Table

When Dusty Fog announced his identity, unless there
was trouble or danger threatening, he frequently took
the chance of being disbelieved. Many people found it
impossible to reconcile his appearance with his
legendary reputation.

That only applied in times of peace.

Such a period existed in the dining-room of the
Longhorn Hotel in Los Cabestrillo. While the waiter
had studied Dusty's two companions with interest, and
a few misgivings, he had barely afforded the Rio Hondo
gun wizard a second glance.

Seated at the center table, with his black Stetson
dangling by its *barbiquejo* on the back of his chair,
Dusty Fog looked like a small, insignificant cowhand;
or horse-wrangler, which was even lower down the
social scale.

Yes, *small*!

Dusty Fog stood a mere five foot six inches in his
high-heeled, fancy stitched boots. While he possessed an
exceptional muscular development, it did not show to
any advantage under his expensive clothing. In fact, he
contrived to make the garments look like somebody's
cast-offs. About his waist was strapped a gunbelt made
by Joe Gaylin. Neither it, nor the matched bone handled
Colt Civilian Model Peacemakers in the cross-draw
holsters, added anything to make him more noticeable.
He had curly dusty-blond hair. In repose, as at that

moment, his face was tanned, fairly handsome, but showed nothing of his true potential.

Each of the men with whom Dusty was sitting caught the eye far more than the small Texan.

Take Waco, at Dusty's left, who had passed himself as 'Matthew "Boy" Caxton' during the visits to Hell.

Something over six foot in height, blond-haired and handsome, he had a powerful young body broadening and strengthening towards full manhood. He had on somewhat dandified cowhand's clothing, purchased in Hell to help his role of an irresponsible outlaw on a spree. There had been men in that town—and other places—who could testify to how well the youngster handled the brace of staghorn-handled 1860 Army Colts which rode his *buscadero* gunbelt.

That Waco was highly skilled in all matters *pistolero* was not surprising. Left an orphan almost from birth in an Indian raid, he had been raised by a rancher with a large family. Leaving his adopted home early, he had drifted the range country; a silent, morose boy with sufficient dexterity in gun-toting to prevent himself from being bullied. He had been working for Clay Allison's wild onion crew when he had first met Dusty Fog. Ever since the small Texan had saved his life, by snatching him from under the CA's stampeding herd,* Waco had changed for the better. Previously he had been proddy, quick to take offense, always too ready, willing and able to protect himself. Treated as a favorite younger brother by the other members of the floating outfit, he had been given an education in many subjects. One of the most important lessons he had learned had been *when*, to add to his knowledge of *how*, to draw and shoot.

Dangerous as Waco had been, and, under the right conditions, still could be, there were many who would have accorded him second place in that to the tall, black-haired, Indian-dark, almost babyishly-innocent featured man called the Ysabel Kid.

* Told in: *TRIGGER FAST.*

Born and raised amongst the Comanche Indians' *Pehnane*—Wasp, Quick Stingers or Raiders—band, of which his grandfather was a war leader of the Dog Soldier lodge, the Kid might have made a famous Indian brave-heart.* However, he had been taken by his father on mustanging, or smuggling, missions along the Rio Grande. There he had acquired a reputation for being a bad *hombre* to cross. In the War Between The States, the Kid and his father, Big Sam Ysabel, had spent much of their time delivering goods—which had been slipped through the Yankee blockade into Mexico—across the international border to the Confederate authorities in Texas. They had also aided Belle Boyd on two of her assignments, including the hunt for Tollinger and Barmain. Bushwhack lead had cut Sam Ysabel down soon after. Hunting for the killers, the Kid had joined Dusty Fog and helped him to deliver Grant's message to Bushrod Sheldon. Then he had agreed to join the OD Connected's floating outfit. His duties were less of cowhand than scout. By birth and training, he was ideally suited for the work.

Not quite as tall as Waco, the Kid was slimmer; but gave the impression of whipcord, tireless strength. He had left off his usual all-black clothing, so that nobody would connect 'Alvin "Comanche" Blood' with Loncey Dalton Ysabel, also known as the Ysabel Kid. Instead, he wore a fringed buckskin shirt, Levi pants and calf-high Comanche moccasins. He had, however, retained his usual armament; in the use of which he was accounted very expert. So his walnut-handled old Dragoon Colt hung in the twist-hand draw holster at the right of his belt and an ivory hilted James Black bowie knife was sheathed on the left.

The trio had the room to themselves. After delivering their food, the waiter had—although they did not know this—slipped away to inform the marshal of their presence.

Having completed their assignment and ensured that

---

* Told in: *COMANCHE*.

the town of Hell would no longer be available for use by
outlaws,* Dusty's party were relaxed. So they paid little
attention to the sound of feet approaching the main entrance of the dining-room. Even the fact that the town's
marshal entered, accompanied by three more men,
caused them no alarm. Two of the newcomers looked
like prosperous Southern gentlemen.

The third was the trio's *amigo*, Mark Counter.

Good old Mark would be able to clear up any misun-
derstandings which the local peace officer might be ex-
periencing.

'Stay put, you *Caxtons, Blood*!' Mark snapped,
flashing out, cocking and lining his Colts at the trio.
'Hands flat on the table.'

On the point of speaking, Waco left the words un-
said.

Just as Mark had anticipated, when deciding upon
how to handle the new development, his *amigos* re-
sponded perfectly. Even the boy, who had been set to
give the whole snap away, played along exactly as the
blond giant wished. Showing alarm, anger, yet a
realization that resistance at that point would be futile
or fatal, Dusty, the Kid and Waco kept in their seats and
slapped their hands, palms down, on the top of the
table.

All of them had noticed the emphasis which Mark
had laid upon the use of their assumed names. Knowing
him, they had read the correct implications from the
words—and even more from his actions. While Mark
might have been playing a joke on them, or upon the
fat, slothful peace officer, before revealing their true
identities, there were limits to how far he would take it.
A man of his great experience, for example, might have
even drawn his guns; but he would never have cocked
the hammers—and be *holding back the triggers*!—in the
course of a joke.

Having taken note of the big blond's words and actions, especially with regard to the triggers of the Colts,

---

* How this was achieved is told in: *GO BACK TO HELL*.

the three cowhands concluded, correctly, that he wanted them to continue being the 'Caxton brothers' and 'Comanche Blood'.

'What's the idea, *hombre*?' Dusty growled, darting glances around as if in search of an avenue of escape.

'You're under arrest, is what!' Flatter announced, suddenly catching up with the rapid turn of events and starting to haul his revolver from its holster.

'Now, now, marshal,' de Richelieu put in. 'Don't let's be hasty.'

'Wha——?' Flatter gurgled, looking baffled.

'You don't know for sure that these young men are the Caxtons and Comanche Blood,' de Richelieu pointed out, shoving the barrel of the marshal's revolver down out of alignment. 'Do you?'

'But, I thought—You mean——!' Flatter spluttered, visions of the reward money floating away from his grasp. 'Cap'n Fog here——.'

'Me?' Mark put in, allowing the triggers to return to a more harmless position. 'I was going on what you told us, marshal. If they should have been those owlhoots, I figure the best way to mention it would be after they couldn't do any arguing.'

'We ain't those fellers you reckon we are!' Waco complained, stirring with an all too casual motion.

'You stay put!' Mark ordered, gesturing at the youngster with his right-hand Colt. 'The other two've likely got sense enough to know better.'

'The marshal tells us you're wanted men,' de Richelieu remarked, as Waco settled into surly immobility. 'Now I've always prided myself on being a good judge of human nature. And I believe that you are nothing more than three young cowboys, out of work and looking for employment.'

'*Work!*' Waco jeered, perfect in his response and part. 'We don't take to——'

'Choke off, *half*-brother!' Dusty commanded angrily, then looked at de Richelieu. 'Yes, sir. That's just what we are.'

'Then you'll be willing to come with me to my ranch?'

'Well——,' Dusty began, fingers moving restlessly.

'Keep your hands still!' Mark snapped. 'It's one thing or the other, *hombre.* You come to work for Colonel de Richelieu. Or the marshal holds you until the Rangers come and say who you really are.'

'You've just hired three men, Colonel,' Dusty drawled. 'Hasn't he, Comanch', half-brother?'

'Me, I'd sooner work cattle'n be locked indoors,' agreed the Kid.

'Matt?' Dusty challenged.

'You're running things, big brother,' Waco submitted sullenly.

'We'll start by having you get up one at a time, shed your gunbelts and move away from the table,' Mark suggested.

'Like hell!' Waco spat.

'Do it, damn you, boy!' Dusty barked.

'I for sure ain't fixing to argue with you, Cap'n Fog,' the Kid went on and stood up, keeping his hands in sight.

'Left-handed and real easy!' Mark warned.

Obeying, the Kid left his gunbelt on the table and moved away from his place. Dusty repeated the dark Texan's actions, picking up and donning his hat in passing.

'Now you,' Mark told Waco.

'Suppose I tell you to go crawl up your butt-end?' the youngster challenged.

'If I do it,' Mark replied, 'you'll be a heap too dead to know.'

'You do like the man says!' Dusty raged. 'Damn it! Don't you have enough sense to know when to yell "calf-rope"?'

'I never took to eating crow!' Waco answered. 'So——.'

'So do like the man says!' Dusty snarled. 'I figure this's for the best.'

'You always figured good enough for us so far, Ed,' drawled the Kid.

'All right, all right!' Waco muttered. 'Happen doing

it gets us hung, I'll never talk to neither of you again.'

Glowering furiously at Mark, the youngster obeyed. Waco did not know what was happening, or greatly care, such was his supreme faith that his *amigos* would be a match for it. So he played along in a manner which was clearly convincing the dudes about his character. They would never guess that he, Dusty and the Kid knew Mark, after the display he was putting on. Waco considered that such a condition might be important.

With the three belts on the table, and their owners standing some feet away, Mark holstered his Colts and walked to hook his rump on the back of what had been Dusty's chair. He sat in a position which would prevent the 'Caxtons' and 'Comanche Blood' regaining possession of their weapons.

'I don't think we need you any more, marshal,' de Richelieu drawled, turning to Flatter.

'Huh?' gulped the peace officer.

'I'd say your boss's saying for you to get the hell out of here,' Waco explained with a grin.

'And I'd say it's easy to see who's the *younger* brother,' Mark drawled. 'The one with the biggest mouth.'

'Yeah?' Waco growled. 'Well I don't——.'

'Shut your hay-hole!' Dusty interrupted viciously. 'Leave him be, Cap'n Fog. He's young——'

'That's been saving him,' Mark answered, 'so far.'

'You'd better explain to the citizens that it's all a mistake and these aren't the outlaws,' de Richelieu told the marshal.

'I'll do that,' Flatter agreed and slouched disconsolately from the room.

'Mind if I ask what your notion is, Colonel?' Dusty inquired. 'You *know* who we are.'

'If it's the Army's reward you're after——', Waco began.

'I could have had it by saying nothing,' de Richelieu pointed out. 'Or shared it with Captain Fog, Major Corbeau and the marshal.'

'Could be you're figuring on the loot,' the Kid

pointed out. 'Which being, you've come *way* too late. We spent it all down in Hell.'

'If you're broke, so much the better,' de Richelieu smiled.

'I've never found being broke better'n anything,' Waco complained.

'In this case, it is. If only for me,' de Richelieu answered. 'You'll be the more likely to take my offer of work. It will give you a safe hiding place from the Army.'

'We've done all right dodging 'em so far,' Waco scoffed, playing the irresponsible, hot-headed hard-case to the hilt. 'Hell, we ain't seed hide nor hair of a stinking blue-belly patrol in weeks. Last 'n's we met up with wound up awful dead.'

'And you think that the Army has forgotten you?' de Richelieu asked. 'They never will.'

'Colonel's right, boy,' Dusty confirmed. 'So we need some place safe to hole up for a spell.'

'Let them have their gunbelts back, Captain Fog,' de Richelieu ordered. 'I think we can trust Mr. Caxton, his brother and Mr. Blood to accompany us.'

'We'll need the belts when we go out of here,' Dusty pointed out, as Mark displayed reluctance. 'And I'll promise you the boy'll behave.'

Leaving the hotel, the party found that a crowd had gathered. Various citizens were still hovering around, hoping for some kind of action. However, the fact that the men emerged in apparent friendliness, and with the three cowhands still wearing their guns, implied that the marshal had been telling the truth.

Collecting the horses at the livery barn, the men were about to mount when de Richelieu reminded Mark that he had not completed his business in town.

'Go and do it, Captain Fog,' the Colonel went on. 'You can catch up with us on the trail.'

'But——' Mark began, darting a meaning look at the three cowhands.

'You can trust them,' de Richelieu assured the big

blond. 'That small one might look like a nobody, but I sense that he's shrewd enough to know when he's well off. And he can keep the other two under control.'

'It's your horse, Colonel, ride it any way you see fit,' Mark drawled. 'Only, was I you, I'd make sure they knew I'm not toting any money on me.'

'I'll do that,' de Richelieu promised.

Leaving Mark and Corbeau behind, de Richelieu accompanied the three Texans across the range. At the man's suggestion, Dusty signaled to his companions to drop behind. Falling a few yards to the rear, the Kid and Waco started up a conversation calculated to further their deception.

'Tell me a little about yourself, Mr. Caxton,' de Richelieu suggested.

'There's not a whole heap to tell,' Dusty replied, wanting a lead as to how he should answer.

'Were you driven to becoming outlaws by Reconstruction?'

'Yankee carpetbaggers took our ranch,' Dusty admitted, using a reason why more than one Texan had been sent on the outlaw trail. 'There wasn't much else a feller could do down here after the War.'

'Why did you decide to rob that Paymaster?'

'He was carrying enough money to make it worth while.'

'Knowing that by doing it, you'd have the whole U.S. Army after you?'

'Something told me they'd not like us doing it,' Dusty admitted cheerfully.

'But you went right ahead.'

'Why, sure.'

'Because you hate blue-bellies?' de Richelieu inquired.

Something in the man's voice supplied Dusty with the required clue on how he should continue.

'I hate their guts. They killed my mother, in a raid early in the War, down to Brownsville. Pa married again. A widow-woman who wasn't our class——.'

'That explains the differences between yourself and your brother.'

'Sure,' Dusty agreed. 'But he's useful to have around and, second to me, he's the fastest I've ever seen with a gun. Anyways, we'd started up ranching on the Panhandle range when peace came. While we was away, carpetbaggers run the boy's maw off, she was killed. We came back from that trail drive and found her grave. Paw went after the carpetbaggers. The State Police got him. Boy 'n' me, we escaped and've been on the dodge ever since.'

'So you've no love for the Yankees?' de Richelieu inquired.

'Colonel,' Dusty replied vehemently. 'I'd kill every blasted one of 'em, given but just a chance.'

'Including Governor Howard?'

'Him more than anybody! It's him who's got the Rangers raising such hell that a wanted man don't hardly dare to go to bed at nights, even in places that used to be safe.'

Instead of commenting, de Richelieu rode on for a time in silence. Dusty also did not speak, but sat as if waiting for the other to continue. The small Texan guessed that the man at his side was debating whether to say anything more. So he decided to prod de Richelieu along.

'These questions about my past're taking us someplace, I'd say,' Dusty drawled.

'They are,' de Richelieu agreed. 'Have you ever heard of the Brotherhood For Southron Freedom?'

'Nope,' Dusty confessed. 'I can't rightly say I have.'

Speaking quickly and with growing excitement, de Richelieu described his organization and its aims. At Dusty's signal. Waco and the Kid ceased their chattering and closed the distance so that they could listen. All of them could now understand why Mark had gone to such lengths to present them as a trio of badly wanted outlaws.

'Just where do we fit in this idea?' asked Waco.

'Would you kill an enemy of the South?' de Richelieu challenged.

'We'd kill *anybody*,' drawled Waco. 'Just so the price's right.'

'Who is it you want killing, Colonel?' Dusty inquired.

'Governor Stanton Howard,' de Richelieu replied. 'With him dead, we'll have the South preparing for war with the Yankees. And this time we'll not be beaten.'

CHAPTER THIRTEEN

Know Her? She's My Wife

'Get down, Miss Boyd, or whoever you are!' Stapler commanded, glaring up as she climbed tiredly from inside the wagon onto the box.

By the time Belle had recovered consciousness, the wagon had been on its way out of Los Cabestrillo. She was in its body, not tied up in any way but guarded by Dunco. Although he had not been hostile, the comic had stated that he would take no chances until the matter of her behavior was settled one way or the other. He had made her remain where she was, but had also told her what had happened after Stapler had knocked her down.

With the connivance of the town's marshal, Stapler had convinced the old telegraphist that Belle was a desperate murderess, badly wanted by the law. Satisfied that the baritone was a Texas Ranger ordered to capture her, the telegraphist had gone about his business. Then Belle had been taken to the barn.

According to Dunco, there had been a heated scene between Sabot the Mysterious and Stapler. The magician had been inclined to discount the baritone's story as no more than jealousy. However, the other men had insisted that Belle must be delivered to the ranch as a prisoner and Colonel de Richelieu informed. Knowing what his fate might be if he refused, the magician had yielded to their demands.

Satisfied that she could not hope to escape in her present weakened condition, Belle had remained passive

during the journey. She had spent her time in throwing
off the effects, or as much as possible, of the attack she
had suffered. She had also tried to think up an explanation for her actions. There had seemed only one
course left open to her. That Sabot would support her
against Stapler. It was not much comfort, but at least it
might produce a respite for her.

Dropping down, Belle tried to read some expression
on Sabot's sallow face. She failed and turned her gaze to
the other men. Something white showed at Downend's
waist. Looking at it, the girl recognized the butt of her
Dance. Clearly Sabot had won one point, refusing to
allow Stapler to keep hold of the weapon. She darted
glances about her, but could see no way in which she
might escape if she made a bid for freedom.

'Let's go see the Colonel,' Mick ordered.

With Stapler gripping her arm, and showing his determination to prevent her from fleeing, Belle allowed herself to be escorted to the big main house. Mick opened
its front door and they entered the hall. Several people
were already present. A beautiful, elegantly-attired
woman, men in the uniforms of Confederate States officers and three cowhands.

'What's all this about, sergeant?' de Richelieu
demanded, seeing from the attitudes of the new arrivals
that something was wrong.

'I don't know, sir,' Mick admitted.

Before any more could be said, Stapler thrust his way
to the front of his party. He shoved Belle ahead of him
and pointed an accusing finger her way.

'This here's Belle Boyd, Colonel,' the baritone
declared. 'I caught her trying to send off a telegraph
message.'

Looking around, Belle felt her heart leap with joy.
Somehow, her request for assistance had been answered
even better than she could have wished it might be. Not
only was Dusty Fog present, but he had his three loyal,
very capable *amigos* available to back his play. They
would make a fighting force to be reckoned with——

Certain facts began to leap through Belle's mind.

Mark Counter was wearing an officer's—a *captain's*—uniform.

Dusty Fog, the Ysabel Kid and Waco had on clothing similar to that described in the newspaper's story. That was made more obvious by the fact that the Kid was not attired in the all black clothing which Belle had been the cause of his first acquiring.

If Belle read the situation correctly, Mark was pretending to be Dusty, while the small Texan and the other two must still be acting as the wanted men.

So how could Belle make herself known to them without admitting her true identity, or spoiling their deceptions?

That problem was taken out of her hands in no uncertain manner.

'You stupid whore!' Dusty roared, leaping towards the girl.

Before Belle, or any of the others, realized what the small Texan was planning, he had lashed the palm of his hand savagely across her face. The slap was not a light one, for Dusty did not dare try to fake his actions. It staggered the girl. Following her, Dusty swung another blow which sent her reeling to fall almost at de Richelieu's feet. Although the attack had hurt, Belle still retained sufficient conscious thought to know what she must do.

'No—no—Ed!' she screeched, watching Dusty stalking in her direction.

'Take it——!' Mark began, when nobody else offered to speak.

'Stand there, big man!' Waco snarled, flashing out his right-hand Colt. 'Brother Ed's got the right to beat up on his woman, happen he's so minded.'

Bending, Dusty took hold and almost tore the shirt from Belle's back as he wrenched her to her feet. Shaking her savagely, he shouted furiously into her tear-smeared, scared face.

'How many times did I tell you about not saying you're somebody famous?' Dusty roared, thrusting her from him. 'Last time it was Belle Starr.'

'Ole Belle whomped her better'n you're doing when she heard about it.' Waco grinned.

'I—I—I—!' Belle whined, stumbling against the wall and huddling herself protectively with both arms covering her head. 'D—don't beat m—me—u—, Ed!'

Nobody in the hall made a move to interfere. While Waco kept his Colt lined on Mark, as if determined that he should not, the others showed no inclination to do other than watch and listen. As Belle sobbed her plea, de Richelieu advanced a couple of paces.

'It seems you know her, Mr. Caxton!'

Spinning on his heel, grateful for the excuse to take no further action, Dusty growled, '*Know* her? She's my wife!'

'*Wife!*' Stapler spat out, sensing that things might turn out badly for him. 'Damn it! She's a dyke.'

'I didn't hear you right, *hombre*,' Dusty said, almost mildly, swinging towards the baritone. 'Now did I?'

Suddenly Stapler found that he was no longer confronted by a small, insignificant cowhand. To him, it seemed that Belle's assailant had taken on size and weight until looking larger than the blond giant in the captain's uniform.

It was one of the moments which Dusty Fog could not be measured in mere feet and inches.

'She—that's what——!' Stapler spluttered, drawing away a pace. 'She told us she was!'

'I—I did it to stop him mauling and chasing me, Ed!' Belle explained.

'I—I wasn't meaning anything by it, Selima!' Stapler apologized. 'Honest, feller, I never went near——.'

'None of them did, Ed!' Belle hastened to assure Dusty. 'I wouldn't let them come near me.'

'That's real lucky for you,' Dusty drawled and the words sounded far more menacing than any amount of a lesser man's bawled out threats.

'And even luckier for the man's'd tried it,' Waco grinned, holstering his Colt. 'Brother Ed's sure particul——.'

'Boy!' Mark barked, joining the youngster in the good work of diverting attention from Belle's admission of her true identity. 'Happen you ever pull down on me again, drop the hammer. Because I'll kill you if you don't.'

'You wanting your chance now?' the youngster challenged, with such ferocity that Belle was almost taken in.

'Would your brother and Mr. Blood help the sergeant with the wagon's team, Mr. Caxton?' de Richelieu put in.

'Go do it, boy!' Dusty commanded.

'Come on, paleface brother,' the Kid went on, advancing and gripping Waco by the arm.

'All right, all right!' Waco spat, wrenching himself free. Continuing with the line he and Mark had followed since their arrival, he went on, 'One day you 'n' me's going to meet and nobody step 'tween us, Captain Fog.'

'That's the day they'll bury you,' Mark answered.

'Hey, how's about coming and giving your husband a loving kiss?' Dusty demanded of Belle, drawing attention from Mark and Waco so that they could let the matter lapse.

Scrubbing her face with her hands, the girl scuttled forward. Once in Dusty's arms, she continued to act perfectly. Although she started by delivering a frightened peck, she changed it into a passionate embrace. Mark studied the byplay and decided, whatever else they might believe, nobody in the hall would accept that Belle had lesbian tendencies.

'I—I didn't know where you'd be at when I came out of the State Penitentiary, Ed!' Belle said hurriedly, but distinctly, wanting Dusty to know something of her 'history'. 'So I've sent a couple of letters—in our code—to the old hide-outs.'

'*That's* what you were doing!' Sabot put in, throwing a vicious, hate-filled glare at the baritone.

'Y—yes, Sabby,' Belle confessed, having been told

by Dunco that Stapler had seen her mailing a letter. She continued with the correct reaction. 'But—but how did you——?'

'Our good friend here told me.' Sabot answered coldly.

'I just figured that Ed and the boys would be useful for the Brotherhood,' Belle explained. 'But I didn't want Strapler a-chasing me again if he heard I wasn't a dyke. So I sent them off without saying anything.'

'So you've been making fuss for my wife, huh?' Dusty said to the baritone.

'Let *me* take care of this, friend,' Sabot suggested, reaching to pluck the Dance from Downend's belt.

'Sabby!' Belle yelled as the magician turned the barrel in Stapler's direction and thumbed back the hammer. 'It's not capped!'

The warning came too late.

Having realized that his plans for humiliating Sabot had failed, Stapler had not been unaware of his own position. The magician would never forgive him and had a vile temper when roused. So the baritone had taken precautions. Ever since the night of the fight in Dallas, he had carried a Colt 'Cloverleaf' House Pistol* in his jacket's right-hand pocket. At the first hint that things were going wrong, he had slipped his fingers around its butt. Jerking it out as Sabot turned the Dance towards him, the baritone aimed from waist level and fired.

Although Sabot heard Belle's warning, its full import did not register until the hammer fell. Nothing but a dull, dry click came to his ears. Even as shock twisted at his sallow face, he saw Stapler's revolver belch flame. Numbing agony tore briefly into the magician as the .41-calibre bullet ripped through his left breast.

'Now for you, you whore!' Stapler screamed, starting to swing the weapon in Belle's direction.

Thrusting the girl away from him, Dusty flung his left hand across to the right-side Colt. Waco and Mark also

---

* Despite its name, the Colt Model of 1871 'Cloverleaf' House Pistol is a revolver.

commenced their draws, determined to protect the girl.
Stapler had less than a minute left to live.

Three heavy calibre revolver shots crashed in a rapid,
ragged volley. Each bullet found its mark in the
baritone. Any one of them would have been fatal. The
combined force of the impacts hurled Stapler backwards. Colliding with the wall, he bounced lifeless to the
floor.

'Sabby!' Belle gasped.

'He's done for,' Captain Raphael declared, kneeling
and making an examination of the motionless figure of
the magician.

'Damn it!' de Richelieu bellowed, his face turning
almost white in rage. 'Why didn't you shoot him more
quickly, Mis—Captain Fog?'

'How was I to know what he aimed to do?' Mark
countered.

'You knew how much our plans depended on Sabot!'
Virginie snapped, glaring furiously at the blond giant.
'So you ought——.'

'It's too late now, Virginie!' de Richelieu said,
making a visible effort to regain control of his
emotions. He looked around for a moment, then
shrugged. 'Will you gentlemen from the show go and
unpack your wagon. You could probably use a meal,
too.'

'Shouldn't we learn more about——Mrs. Caxton
—first?' Virginie asked.

'Do any of you know anything more about her?' de
Richelieu inquired.

'She's always done real good for the Brotherhood,'
the orchestra's leader stated. 'Stapler never liked her,
after she put the knee into his ba—Sorry, lady.'

'But he claimed that she said she was Belle Boyd,'
Virginie remarked, ignoring the apology which had been
thrown her way.

'I heard her,' Dunco said. 'I'm sorry, Selim—Mrs.
Caxton, but you did.'

'That's right, I did,' Belle admitted, having concocted
an acceptable excuse. 'Like I said, I wanted to bring Ed

and the boys into the Brotherhood. So I aimed to get word to them by telegraph. Only they won't send messages in code for ordinary folks. I figured on claiming I was Belle Boyd, working for the Pink-Eyes*, and that way he'd be likely to do it.'

'It worked last time she did it, Brother Ed,' Waco commented.

'Did you hear any of this?' Virginie asked the comic.

'She'd no sooner said she was Belle Boyd than Stapler jumped her,' Dunco replied.

'Are you calling me a liar?' Belle demanded, glaring at the other woman.

'I see you've lost your wedding ring,' Virginie purred.

'Not lost it, sold it,' Belle corrected. 'To get money for traveling while I was looking for Ed. Maybe *you*'d've found another way to do it, but I stop way short of *that*.'

'How dare you!' Virginie hissed.

'How dare you go hinting I'm not Ed's real wife?' Belle blazed back.

'Ladies!' de Richelieu barked. 'Mr. Caxton, please bring your wife into the study. Captain Fog, come with us. Major Corbeau, take the performers to the bunkhouse and settle them in. Major Kincaid, have the bodies removed.'

'Where will Mrs. Caxton sleep?' Virginie purred.

'With my man, of course,' Belle flashed back.

'And his brother and the hal—Mr. Blood?' the Baroness asked.

'Maybe you'd like my knuckles in your mouth!' Belle raged, starting to cock her right fist and move forward.

'Easy, gal!' Dusty ordered, catching her arm and holding her. 'The Baroness didn't mean it that way. Me and the boys've been bunking in the same room upstairs.'

'Maybe your men could sleep at the bunkhouse?' Mark suggested, seeing that Virginie had inadvertently given the solution to one problem.

* Pink-Eye: derogatory name for a member of Pinkerton's National Detective Agency.

'Or in the hayloft at the barn,' the Kid offered. 'I don't take to bedding down among too many folks.'

'Make your own arrangements, gentlemen,' de Richelieu advised. 'Come this way Mr., Mrs. Caxton.'

Going into the study, Dusty was satisfied by what had happened so far. Not only had he saved Belle, but the way was paved for his companions to obtain a greater freedom of movement. Although they had been treated as guests, de Richelieu had insisted that the trio should occupy a room in the house. Having no wish to arouse even slight doubts, they had concurred. However, having Waco and the Kid at liberty and away from the main building might prove advantageous.

Inside the study, de Richelieu seated Belle and Virginie well clear of each other. With the blond giant and the small Texan supplied with chairs, the Colonel brought the meeting to order and commenced:

'Will you please tell us everything, Mrs. Caxton?'

'*Everything?*' Belle countered, throwing a glance at Dusty as if seeking permission.

'Have you something to hide?' Virginie asked, glaring bitter animosity at the slender girl.

'No more than you have, likely,' Belle replied.

'I'd quit riding her, was I you, ma'am,' Dusty advised. 'She might have been born a lady, but she's been mixing in rough company long enough to have forgotten how to make polite cat-talk. Now she goes to scratching, biting and clawing real easy.'

'Belle Starr didn't get it all her own way,' Belle went on. 'She won't have forgotten some of ole Melanie's slaps, I'll bet.'

'We'd like to know more about how you came to be with Sabot,' de Richelieu interrupted firmly.

'It was like I said, I met him while I was looking for Ed, after I'd come out of the State Penetentiary,' Belle replied and continued with a verion of how she had become the magician's assistant so as to travel without paying and to have an excuse for moving from town to town.

'We rigged a code between us before Mellie-gal got

arrested,' Dusty elaborated, when Belle reached the point where she had been caught trying to send the message. 'Knowing how me and the boys feel about the Yankees, she'd figure we'd want to get into the Brotherhood and try to let us know where to come. Looks like I owe you a forgiveness, Mellie-gal. I thought at first you was just trying to pull a confidence trick on that ole feller in Los Cabestrillo.'

'Aw, that's all right, Ed,' Belle answered, gazing at him with starry-eyed love. 'You wasn't to know.'

'There'd been bad blood between the magician and that damned singer, you say?' de Richelieu asked, for Belle had established that in her story.

'Sure,' the girl agreed and turned a suddenly frightened face to Dusty. 'It wasn't because of me, Ed-honey!'

'Professional jealousy, I'm sure,' Virginie purred.

'Some of us're choosey who we bed with,' Belle slashed back, swinging her gaze pointedly between Mark and the Baroness.

For a shot in the dark, the words brought a not unexpected response. Belle saw the anger glow in Virginie's eyes and knew that she had called the play just right. However, although she was seething with a barely controllable rage, Virginie remained in her seat. Once again it fell upon de Richelieu to pour oil on troubled waters.

'Perhaps you would care to retire, Baroness?' he inquired and continued tactfully, 'With the magician dead, we can't make our arrangements.'

'Surely we could put a show on?' Virginie answered.

'Without its star performer?' de Richelieu snorted. 'It was the magician who would have drawn Howard's party to the theatre.'

'I know how to do most of Sabby's tricks,' Belle put in, knowing that one of the other performers might mention her newly-acquired ability.

'*You* do?' Virginie ejaculated.

'Maybe not as well as he did them, but good enough,' Belle replied.

'And the novelty of *you* doing them would cover any slight inadequacies,' de Richelieu breathed. 'Can I see you perform?'

'Tonight?' Belle wailed.

'In the morning will do.'

'I'd need an assistant—a girl——.'

'Perhaps you would do it, Virginie?' de Richelieu suggested.

'*Me?*'

'*Her?*'

Two feminine voices raised at the same instant. Virginie's registered shock and Belle put a load of contempt into her response.

'You reackon the Baroness couldn't learn how to do it, Mellie-gal?' Dusty drawled, grinning.

'Well——,' the girl began, with well-simulated mock hesitancy and contempt.

'I will do it!' Virginie shouted, rising angrily.

'You'd have to dress right for the part,' Belle warned and judged, by the flush which came to the other's cheeks, that Virginie had seen the act.

'If I could get a suitable costume——' Virginie began, accepting the challenge she was sure had been thrown her way by the girl.

'There's one the girl before me left when she quit,' Belle answered. 'It should fit. She was on the overstuffed side—My, what have I just said!'

'I will try it on in the morning!' Virginie snapped and stalked out of the study.

'You sure put a burr under her saddle, Mellie-gal,' Dusty grinned. 'Come on, let's us go to bed.'

'Those are the loveliest words I've heard in years,' Belle purred.

'If your husband has no objections, we will see your performance in the morning,' de Richelieu stated, in a manner that implied the meeting was over.

'I'd admire to see her do it,' Dusty admitted, knowing that they would learn northing more from the Colonel that night.

'You'll be real proud of me, Ed-honey,' Belle purred, eager to discuss the situation in private with Dusty. 'And I'm sure tired.'

While going upstairs, after the Kid and Waco had collected their bed rolls from the room, Belle continued to act like an amorous wife eagerly awaiting her reunion with a very satisfactory husband. She crawled as close as she could to Dusty, nuzzling his cheek, and her hands explored his body in a way which drew a cold, disapproving glare from de Richelieu. She carried on in the same manner until they were inside the room. Allowing Dusty to move away, Belle closed the door and turned towards him. Her fingers touched her cheeks where his slaps had landed.

'Ed-honey,' the girl cooed.

Turning without any inkling of his danger, Dusty found her actions at variance with the tone of voice. Taking aim, she whipped a right swing that connected with the side of his jaw. Such was its force that he shot across the room and went headlong over the bed.

'Ow!' Belle screeched as the crack of her knuckles, arriving against Dusty's jaw, rang out. Timing the rest of her words perfectly, she went on, 'No! Ed! I didn't make sheep's eyes at Captain Fog—Ooof!'

Crossing to the bed, Belle grinned down at the small Texan. Looking dazed, Dusty sat up. He shook his head and gently worked his jaw.

'I never could let anybody slap me without wanting to hit back,' the girl remarked, helping Dusty to rise. 'Perhaps I swung a bit too hard.'

'That depends on whether you wanted to kill me, or just bust my jaw a mite,' Dusty replied. 'Let's talk.'

'We'd best do it in bed,' Belle advised. 'I've an idea we haven't seen the last of her highness tonight.'

As usual, Belle proved to be a good judge of the situation. Insisting that they made everything look right, she and Dusty undressed and climbed into bed. With the lamp out, they lay in each other's arms and talked. Before they could go far in their conversation, the door was opened and light flooded in from the passage. Jerking into sitting positions, they allowed the covers to fall away.

'I'm sorry!' Virginie said, standing in the doorway. 'I've come to the wrong room. How foolish of me. Please forgive me.'

'Just so long as it is the wrong *room*, and not the wrong *night, dear*,' Belle replied, bare torso entwined with Dusty's in the lamp-light. 'Good night.'

CHAPTER FOURTEEN

I'll Scratch Her Eyes Out!

'Whee-Doggie!' Waco enthused, coming to a halt inside the barn and staring in an approving manner at the Baroness de Vautour. 'Now aren't you a fetching picture, ma'am?'

Although Virginie's eyes glowed with annoyance at the youngster's easy familiarity, she forced herself to smile.

It was the fourth day after Belle Boyd's arrival and the Baroness was waiting to commence a further lesson in her duties as magician's assistant. Dressed in the 'harem girl's' costume which had been discarded by the original 'Selima', Virginie filled it even better than had its previous owner. Her rich, sensual body left nothing to the imagination about its shape.

While the Baroness had hated to play a subordinate role, especially to 'Melanie Beauchampaine'—or 'Mrs. Caxton'—she had been compelled to do so. On seeing Belle demonstrate her ability, de Richelieu had expressed his belief that she could do all that was needed. Without explaining more of his scheme, he had dispatched Corbeau and Kincaid to organize a performance for the Governor in San Antonio de Bexar's Variety Theatre. Then he had requested Belle to instruct Virginie in her duties and to rearrange the show to suit its changed status.

Stapler's death had been turned to Belle's advantage. Being short of a singer, and knowing that the Kid had a fine tenor voice, she had persuaded him to replace the dead baritone. That would ensure that Belle had a loyal friend and a capable fighting man at her disposal, even if the other members of the floating outfit were not on hand.

Since that first performance, things had progressed smoothly. Belle and the Texans had continued to play their parts as if their lives depended on doing it; which they did.

Keeping up their pretense of being a devoted, if occasionally violent, couple, Belle and Dusty had slept together every night. That had allowed them to discuss the situation and formulate their plans without fear of being overheard. Apparently the Baroness's first visit had satisfied her, for she did not intrude upon their privacy again.

Dusty and Belle had decided that they must go along with de Richelieu, at least until they had discovered what his plans for dealing with the Governor would be. Having been told of the incident at the Shreveport theatre, Dusty had suggested a line de Richelieu might be contemplating. What they would do if the theory should prove correct had been discussed, without their reaching any firm conclusions.

Belle had achieved little on another matter. When she had discussed 'the Frenchman' with Dusty, he had proposed de Richelieu as the most likely candidate. However, taking advantage of accompanying Mark to the camp, he had obtained the big blond's views. Mark had suggested that Petain, whom he had killed, would have been even more qualified by virtue of his temper and behavior. Even Virginie had been mentioned, by Waco, as a possibility. The Baroness's visit to Mark's room had been cited as an example of her vindictive and ruthless nature. However, Belle had pointed out that Madame Lucienne would have been sure to mention it if her torturer had been a woman.

Much as Belle wanted to solve the mystery, she had refused to allow it to interfere with her main assignment. So she had made no great efforts to learn who was, or had been, called 'the Frenchman'. Possibly, as the name was no longer mentioned, he was already dead. Certainly Waco and the Kid, who mingled freely with the enlisted men, could gain no clue concerning him.

There were, moreover, other things to hold the girl's and the Texan's attention.

In addition to continuing with his training programme for the soldiers, Mark kept up his 'feud' with Waco. With each clash of their temperaments, Virginie had displayed a growing interest in the youngster. She had never been near the blond giant's room since that night when she had come and indulged in passionate love-making. Nor had she shown the slightest hint that it had happened. Learning of the incident, through Dusty, Belle had passed a warning to Mark that the woman probably regretted her actions and hated him more for having caused them. Wanting to know what was on Virginie's mind, Dusty had told Waco to play along with her and see what he could discover.

So far, the youngster had been unable to learn anything. In the hope of getting him better acquainted, Mark had provoked an argument with Virginie at breakfast that morning. It was hoped that she might become more amenable to Waco as a result of the heated scene. Meeting her in the barn was, however, an accident. While Waco and the Kid bedded down in the hayloft, they had been asked to stay away from the building during the day and leave it for the women to use in their rehearsals. The youngster had returned to collect a bandana he had forgotten. Finding Virginie there, he had decided to make the most of his opportunity and try to get better acquainted.

It seemed that the Baroness had notions along the same lines.

'I'm so pleased that you approve,' Virginie smiled, walking forward.

'Can't see anybody's wouldn't, ma'am,' the youngster declared. 'Now me, I don't cotton none to skinny gals like Mellie.'

'Your brother seems to like her.'

'Ed's got a whole slew of foolish notions. Me, when I take to a gal, I want her with more meat to lay hold of, and less temper.'

'You're very discerning,' Virginie smiled, extending her right hand. 'May I use your shoulder for support, my shoe needs adjusting.'

'Feel free any ole time,' Waco offered eagerly, placing his hand under her arm-pit. 'Yes sir. Give me a gal like you any old time. A for-real lady and all.'

'That's not how Captain Fog thinks of me,' Virginie pointed out, leaning closer until her hips rubbed against the front of his body.

'*Him?*' Waco jeered, sliding the arm to her waist. 'He doesn't mean nothing, one way or t'other.'

'They say he's the fastest gun in Texas.'

'*They* say!'

'You don't think so?' Virginie inquired, turning so that her flimsily-concealed bosom rubbed against the youngster's shirt and her arms slid about him.

'I'm game to go and prove it!' Waco boasted. 'Happen *you* was to give the word.'

'You'd be my champion?' the Baroness whispered.

'Try me,' Waco offered and an instant later they were kissing.

And Belle walked in, tossing aside the robe which she had worn from the house to conceal her 'harem' costume.

If the girl had realized what was going on, she would have delayed her entrance and left Waco with a clear field. Before she could withdraw, Virginie had seen her and pulled away from the youngster's arm. So Belle decided that she must act as the woman would be expecting of her.

'My my!' Belle drawled, sauntering forward in a gait that was redolent with mocking offense. 'How romantic.'

'This here's none of your concern, Mellie!' Waco growled.

'You're right,' the girl admitted, but knew that she could not let the incident slip by so casually. 'But I'd've

thought you'd go for somebody a heap closer to your
own age—or is she *mothering* you?'

'Why, you dirty little whore!' Virginie ejaculated,
jumping away from Waco and slapping Belle's face
hard.

If the Baroness had expected the affair to end with
her slap, she was to be rapidly disillusioned. Not only
did Belle object to being struck and not giving anything
in return, she had her character to consider. A girl like
'Melanie Beauchampaine' would not have permitted
such a liberty to be taken and go unpunished.

Catching her balance, Belle whipped around her left
arm. With an explosive 'whack!', her hand imprinted
finger marks on the Baroness's right cheek. Although
the blow snapped her head aside and caused her to reel a
couple of steps, Virginie showed no inclination to withdraw from the fray.

Letting out a screech, the Baroness lunged at Belle.
Side-stepping, the girl allowed her to rush by. Pivoting
smoothly, Belle delivered a kick to the woman's shapely
rump, sending her sprawling belly down across a bale of
hay.

'You wait until I tell Ed what's happened, Matt
Caxton!' Belle yelled, turning as if she meant to go and
do it.

Rising from the bale, face wild with anger and
humiliation, Virginie hurled herself forward. She went
after Belle like a football player making a tackle.
Locking her arms around the girl's slender waist, she
used her supperior weight to sweep Belle from her feet.
They hit the floor together, hands diving into hair.
Screaming, squealing curses, shedding strips of their
flimsy garments, they rolled over and over in an inex-
tricable tangle of waving arms and legs.

About to intervene, Waco realized that doing so
would be out of character for 'Matt Caxton'. A
youngster with 'Matt's' irresponsible outlook would
never think of interrupting what he would regard as an
enjoyable spectacle. If there had been any real danger to
Belle, Waco would not have hesitated. Figuring that

that girl could more than hold her own, he stood back. The noise they were making, especially if he helped out a mite, would soon enough attract attention and bring other men on the run. Sure enough, he could hear startled yells from off by the house.

'Go to it, ma'am!' Waco whooped. 'Give her more than Belle Starr did.'

At that moment, Virginie appeared ideally situated to follow the advice. In the upper position, with Belle's hips straddled between her shapely thighs, she had her fingers knotted into the girl's shortish hair. Bracing her neck desperately, the girl struggled to reduce the force with which her attacker was trying to pound her head on the floor. Groping wildly, Belle scrabbled with her fingers at the Baroness's back. While the girl's nails were neither long nor sharp, they hurt and ripped apart the upper section of Virginie's 'harem' outfit.

Bracing her feet and shoulders on the floor, Belle arched her body upwards in an attempt to displace Virginie. It was a mistake. Slipping sideways, the woman slid her left leg under the girl's body. Instinct might be guiding Virginie's response, but it did so in an effective manner. With the girl's slender midsection clamped between her legs, she crossed her ankles and started to apply a crushing, savage leverage.

Belle croaked in agony, grasping at Virginie's columnar thighs with both hands as she tried to relieve the constricting pressure. Realizing that she could not, the girl changed her point of attack. Both hands flew to Virginie's scantily protected bosom, thumbs and fingers hooking deep into the mounds of flesh. The Baroness let out a screech of torment. Numbing agony ripped through her, causing her to untangle her legs hurriedly. Still retaining her grips, Belle writhed free. Turning the frantically struggling woman over. Belle crawled to pin her down with a knee jammed against her pelvic region.

Watching Virginie's desperate struggles, Waco knew that she was as good as beaten. He wondered if he should intervene, before Belle's anger made her go too far.

Dusty, de Richelieu, the Kid, Corbeau and Kincaid burst into the barn. Skidding to a halt, they stared at the embattled women for a moment. The small Texan recovered first. Hurrying forward, he hooked his hands under Belle's arm-pits and dragged her backwards from her victim. In doing so, he completed the ruin of half of the Baroness's costume. As Belle's fingers were dragged from their grip, they brought the upper section away with them. Sitting up, Virginie tried to grab her departing assailant. Before she could do so, Waco and Corbeau had caught her by the biceps and hauled her to her feet.

'Let me at her!' Belle screamed, struggling to get free.

'I'll kill her!' Virginie shrieked, trying to shake off the man. She was oblivious of her naked bosom, barely concealed lower limbs, or anything but the equally disheveled and bedraggled girl.

Throwing Belle from him, Dusty propelled her ino a hay-filled but otherwise unoccupied stall. Following her, he hoped that she was not in such a state of fury that she would be unaware of her actions. Anger glared in her eyes as she rose and moved towards the small Texan. Then it cleared. Yet, to all other appearances, she was still in a raging temper.

'I'll scratch her eyes out!' Belle screamed, darting forward.

'Get her to hell out of here!' Dusty roared, restraining Belle who was continuing to act in a convincing manner. 'Throw her into the horse-trough to cool her off. I'll do the same with Mellie.'

Suddenly Virginie became aware of just how little clothing remained. With a shriek of mortification, she stopped struggling and clutched both hands to her bosom. Shaking herself free from the men's grasp, she fled out of the barn.

Left in possession of the battlefield, as it were, Belle allowed Dusty to shake her out of her 'anger'.

'Don't hit me, Ed!' the girl wailed. 'She started it!'

'And if we didn't need you both all pretty and not

marked up, I'd have let you settle it all the way,' Dusty answered.

'God!' de Richelieu raged. 'The stupid bitches! Now what the hell do we do?'

'About what?' Belle gasped.

'The idea,' Dusty answered savagely. 'These gents have just got back from San Antone and the theatre's ready.'

'She started it!' Belle insisted. 'She hit me first!'

'By God, I know who'll hit you *next*, happen you don't shut up!' Dusty warned. 'Colonel. Happen you can make the Baroness go through with it, Mellie here'll do her part.'

'I wo——!' Belle began.

'Oh yes you will!' Dusty snarled, swinging to face her. 'Or I'll beat you black and blue. Now get going to the house and clean yourself up. Once she's done it, Colonel, we'll meet you in the study and talk this thing out.'

Two hours later, washed, hair combed neatly, wearing a dress and with only a swollen top lip to show that she had been in a fight, Belle went with Dusty into de Richelieu's study. While she had been bathing and changing, they had decided that they must go along with de Richelieu's plan, learn what it was, then figure out how to counter it. They found Corbeau, Kincaid, the Kid and Waco present. The youngster stood protectively beside Virginie's chair and scowled at Belle. The Baroness looked the same as she usually did, except for her blackened left eye.

'Go on!' Dusty growled, nudging Belle with his elbow.

'Do I have to?' the girl demanded, then showed alarm. 'All right! All right, if that's how you want it, Ed.' She crossed the room to halt in front of Virginie. 'I'm sorry for whip—for what happened, Baroness.'

'So am I!' the woman gritted.

'And I'd admire for you to help me in the show,' the girl continued, after a pleading glance in her 'husband's direction and receiving a warning glare in return.

'Very well, I'll do it,' Virginie promised, almost duplicating Belle's actions in her hurried gaze at de Richelieu. 'We'll forget our differences for the good of the Cause.'

'And now you wish to know what this is all about, ladies and gentlemen,' de Richelieu guessed, as Belle rejoined Dusty and they sat down.

'I for sure do,' Waco drawled eagerly. 'Virginie here couldn't tell me no more than it was important and we'd set a burr under the Yankees' saddles.'

'Matthew was good enough to come and offer his apologies for what happened at the barn!' the Baroness put in, darting a worried glance at de Richelieu. 'I told him a little.'

'And I'll tell him more,' de Richelieu promised. 'At the performance your wife and her people will put on for the Governor, Mr. Caxton, we intend to create an incident that will bring the people of Texas flocking to our side. Not just Texas. Once the word is spread of what is happening, the whole of the South will rise again.'

'How'll that happen?' asked Dusty.

'I've seen both you and your brother hit a small target at long range with your handguns,' de Richelieu replied, referring to a display of fast drawing and accurate shooting which Dusty and Waco had given on their way out to the ranch. 'Could you do the same on a man?'

'Even easier,' Waco stated. 'He'd be a bigger mark.'

'I want him killed,' de Richelieu pointed out.

'One or more .44 balls anywhere between the neck and knee-bone'll do that,' Waco declared. 'Who's the man?'

'Governor Stanton Howard,' de Richelieu replied. 'Mrs. Caxton and the Baroness will do the disappearing lady trick. But when your wife opens the box's door to show it's empty, you and your brother will leap out and start shooting.'

'At the Governor, in his box,' Dusty drawled.

'Of course,' de Richelieu confirmed.

'Where he'll be with Cap'n Fog and them other

ranchers,' Waco went on. 'Any one of them's fast enough to make blue windows in us as soon as we pop a cap.'

'They won't be armed,' de Richelieu replied. ' "Captain Fog" will see to that.'

'What do we gain by doing it, even counting we get away alive?' Dusty asked. 'Howard's a right popular man. Killing him won't make folks in Texas feel friendly towards the Brotherhood.'

'That's true,' de Richelieu conceded. 'But they won't be blaming the Brotherhood. All their blame will go to the Yankees.'

'How'd you make that out?' Dusty asked.

'Because of the soldiers who will appear and arrest the ranchers straight after the shooting,' de Richelieu replied. 'When it's learned that they've shot Pierce and the others "trying to escape", everybody will believe that the Yankees were behind the killing of Howard——.'

'Because he's doing such a good chore of setting Texas back on its feet,' Dusty finished for de Richelieu and, sounding far more enthusiastic than he felt, he continued. 'By cracky, Colonel, I do believe it could work.'

CHAPTER FIFTEEN

She Wants Me to Kill You, Mark

'Lordy-lord, Dusty!' Belle breathed, lying alongside the small Texan in bed. 'Did you ever hear such a cold-blooded plot?'

'It's a dilly for sure,' Dusty agreed, thinking of the discussion and consultation which had been carried out in the study as de Richelieu had enlarged on his plan to plunge the United States into a second civil war. 'What do we do about it, Mellie-gal.'

'I hate that name,' Belle said tartly, then became serious. 'Get out, fetch back a regiment of cavalry and break up the Brotherhood seems the obvious answer.'

'Trouble being, it's too damned obvious,' Dusty pointed out. 'There's no garrison closer than a three day ride; and that's even after we've got to town, or over to San Antonio to send a telegraph message.'

'How long would it take us to reach San Antonio?'

'Half a day with the wagon, less just on horses.'

'How *quickly* could it be done?'

'Riding Comanche-style, Lon could make it there and back in a night,' Dusty answered. 'But, good as you are, Mellie-gal, you couldn't do that. In fact, I'm willing to bet Mark, Waco and I couldn't either.'

'But Lon could,' Belle breathed.

'Given just half a chance, and two good horses to ride relay. Do you see this the same way I see it, Mel —Belle?'

The changing of the girl's name came as she registered her disapproval in a painfully effective manner.

'Such as, *Ed-honey*?' Belle purred.

'Hey! No fair grabbing me like that, I can't do it back,' Dusty protested. 'And stop fooling around, li'l wife.'

'How *do* you see it, Dusty?'

'We have to let it go through, de Richelieu's notion, I mean. And stomp on it away from here.'

'That would be terribly risky,' Belle pointed out.

'So would handling it any other way,' Dusty countered. 'If we let Lou go and send the message, de Richelieu's smart enough to figure out what's happened. In which case, I don't reckon we'll leave here alive. Even if he doesn't cotton on to us, just one slip on the Army's part, one tiny little word that they're coming, and there'll be a battle here that could do all he wants.'

'We could save ourselves by all slipping away.'

' "Mellie Caxton" might think that's the answer, but Belle Boyd knows it's not,' Dusty drawled. 'As soon as they found we'd gone, the leaders of the Brotherhood would figure out where and why. Then they'd have their men scatter and be over the border into Mexico before the Army laid hands on them.'

'And leave them free to try other, even worse, schemes,' Belle breathed. 'I wish I wasn't smart like that girl you mentioned. Then maybe I'd not be afraid.'

'There's not many——.'

'Dont start saying "many women", Dusty Fog!' Belle interrupted furiously. 'Not in that smug, superior male tone.'

'I'm right sorry, ma'am,' Dusty apologized. 'So get your cotton-picking hands off!'

Only by the lighter exchanges could the girl and the small Texan relieve the tension that was rising inside them. Both had seen the worst effects of the War Between The States and its aftermath. So they knew the full deadly peril of their present situation.

'Have you any ideas how we do it, Dusty?' Belle wanted to know.

'Some. It'll take planning, be risky as hell, but it could work.'

'Thank God you're here!' the girl whispered, moving closer to Dusty as he completed a recital of his plan. 'It has to work and I'm praying it will. If I'd been alone——.'

'Would you rather've had the three regiments of cavalry?' Dusty inquired, recollecting the message which Belle had mentioned sending.

'I don't think I would, *right now*,' Belle replied.

'They'd sure crowd the bed a mite,' Dusty grinned and kissed the girl. 'I like this man's Army. In the Texas Light Cavalry I never got to sleep with a full colonel.'

In both the Confederate and U.S. Secret Service, Belle had been awarded the rank of colonel to help her deal with military personnel on her assignments.

'Well, I was always for democracy,' Belle replied. 'But I never carried associating with my inferiors *this* far, Captain Fog.'

'What about when this is over, Belle?' Dusty asked as her mouth found his.

'You'll go your way and I'll go mine,' the girl answered. 'I'm not cut out to make anybody, especially a nice feller like you, an ever-loving wife.'

'Lady,' Dusty breathed, after their long embrace. 'You could've fooled me on that score.'

Next morning, after breakfast, Mark Counter entered the center cubicle of the three-holder back-house. While Waco and the Kid occupied the end compartments, Dusty had just quit the one in the middle. Closing its door, Mark picked up the sheet of paper which Dusty had left on the floor. There was sufficient light let in by the decorative ventilation holes for him to read the message on the paper.

'Whooee!' Mark breathed. 'So that's the notion, huh?'

'Didn't the Colonel tell you?' asked the Kid.

'Only that they're planning to stop the show and

make a patriotic speech,' Mark replied. 'Counting on Stanton Howard showing how loyal he is to the Yankees by ordering them to stop, or trying to have them arrested.'

'They figure you believe it?' Waco inquired.

'De Richelieu put up a mighty convincing argument,' Mark answered. 'In the end, I let on like I believed it. So they're going to have you and "Brother Ed" pop up on the stage, gun down the Governor and "Captain Fog", huh, boy?'

'Why, sure,' Waco agreed. 'Figuring that, by doing it and laying all the blame on the Yankees, Ole Devil'll be riled and state out loud and clear he's backing the Brotherhood For Southron Freedom up to the Green River and on to the hilt.'

'And I'm supposed to set them up for the kill?' Mark growled.

'That's just what you're going to do,' the Kid agreed.

'Found something out last night about Virginie,' Waco remarked, sounding just a mite too casual.

'She don't have any hair on her chest,' suggested the Kid, referring to a discovery the youngster claimed to have made about a young lady of his acquaintance in Mulrooney, Kansas, on their first visit.

'That too. She sure is one demanding woman, I tell you. But she's took quite a shine to me——.'

'Now *there's* a gal with what I'd call real good taste,' Mark said dryly, knowing there must be more to Waco's story.

'Better'n you figure,' Waco drawled. 'She wants me to kill you, Mark.'

'Somebody's coming!' warned the Kid, then raised his voice. 'Hey, Matt, is there any paper in your place?'

'You want for me to fetch it with my pants round my knees?' Waco bellowed back. 'Let me get through and I'll fetch you a page from the dream book* that's got pictures of gals in things us boys never see 'em wearing.'

Reading through Dusty's instructions, after the Kid

---

* Dream-book: mail order catalogue; old issues were used in place of toilet rolls.

and Waco had taken their noisy departure, Mark completed his other reason for paying the visit. He wondered how the small Texan would cope with the latest developments. The scheme Dusty had laid out was risky, dangerous, but could work.

If it failed——

Mark did not care to contemplate the results of failure.

Making use of the sheet of paper, so that nobody would be likely to retrieve and decipher it, he let it flutter into the hole. Hitching up his riding breeches, he adjusted his clothing and stepped from the cubicle.

After Mark had left to carry out a final day's training, before he set off to join the Governor's party at San Antonio de Bexar, de Richelieu took Dusty, the Kid, Waco and Belle into the house's cellar. It was their first visit, for the entrances had always been kept locked, and it handed them quite a surprise. The big room held several boxes, with the Henry rifles which had brought Belle on to the Brotherhood's trail. French *Chassepots* and a plentiful supply of ammunition for both types of weapon.

The rifles alone did not create the biggest shock. That came from the sight of a strange-looking, wheel-mounted, multi-barreled gun.

'What is it, a Gatling?' asked Waco, moving forward.

'A Montigny *Mitrailleuse*,' de Richelieu corrected. 'The weapon which, had it been used correctly, would have defeated the Prussians despite their discipline.'

'Looks lighter than any Gatling I ever saw,' Dusty commented. 'I've seen a few, around Army posts.'

'It is,' de Richelieu enthused. 'On this carriage, one man can traverse it.'

'Which, way you're talking, didn't do the Frogs no good at all,' commented the Kid.

'That was because they didn't appreciate how it should have been used,' de Richelieu replied. 'They insisted on using them as artillery pieces, even this light model, instead of using them as infantry support arms.'

'That's how you'd've done it, huh, Colonel?' Dusty inquired.

'That's how I wanted to do it,' de Richelieu agreed. 'But I was overruled by the short-sighted High Command. And so they lost the War. If I'd had my way, gentlemen——Well, that's in the past. When we declare Secession, the Armies of the Confederate States will use their *Mitrailleuses* correctly, allowing our infantry to lay down such a volume of fire that no foot or cavalry assault can penetrate it in an attack.'

A far-sighted professional soldier, de Richelieu had assessed correctly the manner in which a machine gun should be used. He was many years ahead of his time.

'You mean you've got more of these guns?' Dusty inquired, indicating the *Mitrailleuse.*

'They'll be made available when we need them,' de Richelieu replied. 'And how is your problem coming along, Mrs. Caxton?'

'Both our outfits are ruined,' Belle replied, jerking her gaze from the machine gun's protective shield. 'They weren't meant for anything so strenuous as we went at it.'

'Can't Pieber do anything?' de Richelieu growled.

'It would take a real magician to do anything with what's left,' Belle replied. 'Your man doesn't have any suitable material, for one thing.'

'By God?' de Richelieu blazed. 'If you two——'

'I've come up with an idea——' Belle began hurriedly.

'It was *Virginie's* notion,' Waco interrupted indignantly.

'All right, all right!' Belle yelped, glaring at her "brother-in-law". '*We* got to talking it out after breakfast and she came up with this notion. See, neither of us were too happy about wearing those flimsy "harem" outfits on the stage. They'd be hell to ride in if things go wrong and we have to light out in a hurry.'

'That's something we never took into account, Colonel,' Dusty remarked.

'It's not a thing *men* would take into account,' Belle

declared. 'So we—all right, she figured we should wear something that we *could* ride in.'

'You'll need something fancy, to hold the crowd's attention, Mrs. Caxton,' de Richelieu warned. 'Good as you are——'

'Hell! I know I'm not set to make a steady living out of being a stage magician,' Belle put in. 'So *we*——,' she glared defiantly at Waco, who let the word go by unchallenged, 'figured out our costumes. We're going to be two cowgirls.'

'In Stetsons, Levi pants and all?' Dusty drawled.

'Stetsons, sure,' Belle confirmed. 'But we picked something a mite more eye-catching for the rest of it. We've got the tailors cutting up one of the "Dutchess's" black satin frocks, to make us a pair of blouses that will knock your eyes out, and *real* tight riding breeches. Then we'll have riding boots and gunbelts, so everybody will know we're cowgirls.'

'I see,' de Richelieu drawled. 'But how about your billing?'

'Mr. Corbeau just said I was a lady magician, he told us when we asked,' Belle replied. 'So we'll have it announced that it's my first performance and the beginning of a new act. That ought to do it.'

'Virginie's sure one smart gal!' Waco praised. 'She comes up with most of the answers——.'

'It's still me who has to do the tricks!' Belle snapped and stormed out of the cellar.

'You and your big mouth!' Dusty growled at his "brother". 'If you rile Mellie so she busts up this deal, I'll fix your wagon for good.'

'I'll mind it,' Waco promised sullenly and followed the girl.

Locking up the cellar, after the girl's and the Texans' departure, de Richelieu frowned. Clearly Virginie had been working on the suceptibilities of young 'Caxton'. De Richelieu wondered why. Completely ruthless and immoral, she was never promiscuous. As long as he had known her, she had never sought men out merely to satisfy her lust; but only to serve more material ends.

The daughter of a once wealthy Yankee business-man—of Germanic origin—who had been arrested and ruined for trading with the Confederate States during the War, Virginie had fled to Europe. She had married the aged, very rich Baron de Vautour. Although his estates were situated on the German border of the Alsace, the Baron had been violently pro-French. Despite Virginie's warnings and suggestions, the Baron had refused to change his allegiance to the Prussians when the clouds of war had gathered. His stubbornness had cost him his life and threatened to lose something which Virginie had held even more dear. As part of the consequences of defeat, France had ceded control of the Alsace to Germany and the de Vautour lands were to have been confiscated.

Hearing of this, Virginie had made an arrangement with the Prussians. For permission to retain her lands, and a suitable salary, she would become a spy. Showing more imagination than might have been expected, they had agreed.

It had been Virginie who had located de Richelieu and offered aid. He had been unable to learn from whom she had heard of him and his ambitions. Nor did he yet know if she was working for the Prussian Government, or upon the behalf of wealthy speculators. Whoever held the purse strings, they had been lavish in their payments. That was one of the reasons why de Richelieu had not delved more deeply into their identities. As long as they helped with his dreams of liberating the South, he did not care where the money came from.

Whatever Virginie might have in mind for young 'Caxton', de Richelieu figured she was cold-bloodedly calculating enough to avoid it interfering with their grand plan.

'Well,' Waco drawled, lounging at ease on the bed in Belle's and Dusty's room. 'Now we know who's behind the Brotherhood.'

'Who'd that be?' the girl inquired innocently, darting a glance from the youngster to Dusty and the Kid.

'There's some, being *real* smart, "sister-in-law", who might figure French *Chassepot* rifles and the *Mitrailleuse* gun add up to them coming from England or maybe Mexico——.'

'Or even Prussia?' Dusty put in.

'So you-all saw it too, Ed-honey?' Belle asked. 'I didn't know that you understood German.'

'I don't——!' Dusty began.

'Way he cusses a man out, he doesn't need but good old U.S.,' Waco growled.

'Admit it, boy,' suggested the Kid. 'You've missed something and your "kinfolks" haven't.'

'All right,' the youngster sighed. 'What was it?'

'If you hadn't been so busy siding with your rich sweetie against your loving kin,' Belle answered, 'you might have seen the writing on the gun's shield. I don't read much German, but I made it out as, "Property of the King of Prussia".'

'Not being smart, like the rest of my kin,' Waco drawled, rising and crossing the room, 'I don't even know where Prussia is. Maybe Virginie'll tell me. Hey. What do you call a feller who marries a Baroness?'

'A stupid knobhead is one name,' Belle answered. 'I could think of worse.'

'Brother Ed,' Waco drawled, making sure that he had the handle turned and the door on the point of being opened. 'You sure married beneath yourself with that gal.'

With that, the youngster beat a hasty retreat. Belle lowered Dusty's hat, having snatched it up to throw, watched the door close and chuckled.

'That Waco!' she ejaculated. 'What a boy!'

'He'll likely make a hand,' the Kid drawled, delivering the cowboy's supreme accolade, but with reservations. 'Happen he lives that long. Company he keeps, he could get lucky and be hung young.'

'I don't want to be the kind of wife who complains about her loving husband's friends, Ed,' Belle said, eyeing the Kid pointedly.

'Humor him, Mellie-gal,' Dusty advised, safe in the

knowledge that the girl would not show her disapproval
of the name in the same way she had the previous night.
At least, not while the Kid was present. 'He's got to take
a long ride tonight.'

'Can you make San Antonio and back before morning, Lon?' Belle inquired.

'Why, sure,' replied the Kid. 'There're three hosses at
the corral's'll do it easy.'

'You won't be using your own mount?' the girl asked.

'No ma'am,' the Kid declared. 'For one thing, it'd be
a sure giveaway.'

'What's the other reason?' Belle wanted to know.

'The hosses I use won't be fit for work for days,' the
Indian-dark Texan explained. 'If at all.'

'You're sure that Counter will go through with his
part in it?'

Hearing Virginie's words, Waco decided against
knocking at her door and announcing his presence. The
passage was deserted, so he knew that he could listen to
the conversation without being interrupted or detected.

'Yes,' came de Richelieu's hard tones in reply. 'I
don't think he was so favorably disposed towards
acting as Fog's decoy as he pretended.'

'That's what I thought,' Virginie admitted, having
the type of mentality which refused to accept somebody
else could reach a conclusion that she had not already
formed. 'It must be galling to a man like him to have to
pretend he's somebody else.'

'Yes. And it must have been even more galling to
know that all the good work he is doing with the enlisted
men is being credited to Captain Fog.'

'Does Counter know what we're planning—all of it,
I mean?'

'Only that we'll interrupt the meeting. But he's smart
enough to have figured it's something bigger than that.
Perhaps he even guesses correctly.'

'It could even be that he's looking forward to continuing being ''Captain Fog'',' Virginie purred. 'He's
often commented how he never gets such good treatment as himself.'

'That's why I trust him,' de Richelieu admitted.

'Where will he be at the theatre?' Virginie inquired, just a shade too casually.

'In the box with the other ranchers' foremen, so that he can make sure none of them are armed,' de Richelieu answered. 'Why are you so interested in him? I thought your tastes went to *younger* men.'

'Young Caxton will be useful——.'

'To the Brotherhood—or to you, Virginie?'

Hearing footsteps on the stairs, Waco concluded that he would be unable to continue eavesdropping. Which was a pity, as he had hoped that he might discover why the Countess had formed her attachment to him. While he had a good idea of one reason, she could have had others. Knocking at the door, as if he had just arrived, he turned its handle and strolled in without waiting for an invitation.

'Why, Matthew,' Virginie greeted, lips smiling but eyes showing her irritation at his behavior. She darted a glance at de Richelieu. 'The Colonel and I were just talking about the plan.'

'Why, sure, Virginie-gal,' the youngster drawled cheerfully, his whole attitude hinting that he doubted if anybody could replace him as the center of her affections. 'I was wondering if you'd care to come riding—or something?'

Virginie was saved the trouble of making excuses to evade the issue. There was a knock at the door and Pieber entered, carrying her stage costume.

CHAPTER SIXTEEN

She Tried to Kill Me!

With a few slight, but necessary, changes, de Richelieu's plan went off practically exactly as scheduled.

No matter who had devised them, Belle Boyd's and Virginie de Vautour's costumes had carried out their functions in a most satisfactory manner. Or so Mark Counter had concluded as he watched the performance from the box which held the other ranchers' foremen. Belle's Dance rode in the holster of her gunbelt. Improvised from a military weapon belt, Virginie's rig carried a fancy-looking, pearl-handled Lefauchex pinfire revolver in its now flapless holster.

That everything went as smoothly as it did, right up to the 'deaths' of Governor Howard, the member of his staff who had dressed in range clothes and posed as Dusty fog, and Mark, was a tribute to the small Texan's organizing ability—and the part played by the Ysabel Kid.

Few, if any, white men could have done what the Kid had achieved.

Extracting the three selected horses from the corral, at night and so quietly that the occupants of the nearby buildings had not been disturbed, was quite a feat in itself. The fact that the Kid had already spent time in gaining the animals' confidence did little to diminish the praise he had deserved for his efforts.

Having passed through the ring of vedettes without being detected, the Kid had set off on his assignment.

Riding as only a Comanche *tehnap** could, he had made
very excellent time in covering the forty-odd miles to
San Antonio de Bexar. On his arrival, he had located
and obtained an interview with the Governor.
Delivering Dusty's message and suggestions, he had
received Howard's promise that everything would be
done as the small Texan requested. With that assurance,
the Kid had made the return journey to the ranch before
daybreak. He had ridden six horses—three borrowed
from the Governor's party—into the ground, but he had
done his share in averting the peril of another civil war.

Although de Richelieu had cursed when the loss of the
three horses had been reported, he did not even come
close to suspecting what had happened. The Kid had
given a convincing display of tracking the 'thieves',
finally losing the 'trail' on some hard, stony ground.
Having nobody else who could handle the sign-reading,
de Richelieu had accepted the Kid's excuse without
question. He had vetoed a more lengthy search on the
grounds that there would be insufficient time before the
show left for its engagement in San Antonio de Bexar's
Variety Theatre.

The conspirators' journey to San Antonio had been
uneventful. Leaving the others about a mile clear of the
outskirts, Mark had ridden on alone. Meeting the
Governor, he had been pleased to discover that all of
Dusty's arrangements were being respected. Not only
had Shanghai Pierce, Miffin Kennedy and Richard King
willingly given their co-operation, but the town marshal
had placed his entire department at the small Texan's
disposal.

De Richelieu had not accompanied the party. There
had been considerable discontent amongst the men at
the camp. Already many of them were becoming disen-
chanted by Mark's strenuous training programme. So
they had been ripe to accept a rumor—started by the
Kid and Waco at Belle's suggestion—that the
Brotherhood was to be disbanded. So cleverly had the

* Tehnap: an experienced warrior.

Texans done their work that a furious de Richelieu had been unable to track down the source of the fabrication.

As he would be using his most fanatical followers as the 'soldiers' who were to 'arrest' and murder the ranchers, de Richelieu had known that his chief support in the camp would temporarily be absent. If the restless, disgruntled men saw that all the leaders had gone, they might conclude that the rumor was true and desert *en masse*. So de Richelieu had reluctantly decided that he must remain at the ranch. That would offer a convincing argument against the Brotherhood disbanding. He would leave the 'arrests' to Corbeau, Kincaid and Raphael.

On the evening of the show, all had been made ready. Not only on the Brotherhood's side. Dusty had suggested certain precautions in his message to Governor Howard and they had been implemented. Every patron entering the theatre had been disarmed and searched for concealed weapons by the marshal and his deputies; ostensibly as a measure against interference with the smooth running of the conference. That had only applied to the people who used the main entrance. Going in by the stage door, Dusty and Waco were still in possession of their Colts.

To cover Dusty's absence, Howard had selected one of his most trusted secretaries. An accomplished performer in amateur theatricals, the young man had thrown himself whole-heartedly into the role. Dressed in a suitable manner, he had played his part admirably and had given a stirring display of getting 'shot'.

All had gone without a hitch. The cross-talk duo had been well received, garnering laughter and applause by their rapid flow of patter. Looking more worried and frightened than when he had set off to 'borrow' the three horses—or handle even riskier chores—the Kid had sung his songs to an appreciative audience. He had left the stage, swearing in three languages, and stating that he would never again allow himself to be talked into such a nerve-wracking position.

If Belle and Virginie had been anxious, or concerned

by performing before an audience, it had not shown. Although there had been a couple of slight fumbles, the women had covered them up in a professional manner. Certainly, in view of Belle's and the Baroness's appearances in the 'cowgirl' outfits, the primarily male audience had not been inclined to be over-critical.

Inside the box, as soon as the door had closed, Virginie stamped twice on its floor. Instantly the section had slid down silently and swiftly through the open trapdoor over which the structure had been positioned. On reaching the floor of the basement, the woman jumped out of the open-sided framework. She made way for Dusty and Waco to enter, directing a pointed, conspiratorial glance at the youngster as he went by. Having delivered what she hoped would be a reminder to Waco of his added duty, she withdrew.

As soon as the Texans were aboard, the Kid, Dunco, Downend and the man who usually conducted the show's orchestra—they were using the Variety Theatre's regular musicians that night—manipulated the ropes to send the platform shooting upwards again.

Backing away slightly, Virginie watched them go. Hatred drove any semblance of beauty from her face. It would have given warning that she planned something evil, if any of the men had happened to look around. Drawing the Lefauchex, she stared with fixed intensity at where the platform was once more forming the floor of the magic box.

Shots roared overhead!

Almost before they had received the foot-stamping signal, Dunco, Downend and the musician started the platform on its return journey. With a yell, the Kid tightened his grip on the ropes. So did the others, but the over-loaded elevator was descending somewhat faster than had been anticipated. It landed with a crash and precipitated its occupants into the basement.

'Get the hell out of here!' Dusty roared, striving to retain his footing and acting as if the deed had been in earnest.

Stumbling in the opposite direction to Dusty and Waco, Belle saw something that handed her one hell of a shock!

Not far away, Virginie stood looking as mean as all hell!

Raising the Lefauchex, the Baroness aimed it at the girl!

Instead of trying to halt her stumbling steps, Belle threw herself forward even faster. Her right hand turned palm-outwards as she went, curling around the Dance's ivory handle and twisting the weapon from its holster.

Cracking viciously in the confines of the basement, Virginie's Lefauchex vomited its bullet while she was still trying to correct her aim.

Lead made an eerie 'splat!' sound as it whipped by Belle's head; so close that she felt its wind stir her hair. Refusing to be thrown into panic, she skidded to a halt and swiveled to face the peril. Already drawn, the Dance was thrust into instinctive alignment at waist-level. Belle adopted the gunfighter's crouch which she had learned from Dusty Fog and it served her as well as it had him on numerous occasions.

Down flashed the Dance's hammer. Its .36-calibre ball took Virginie in the left breast as the Baroness tried to improve on her first effort. She reeled, tottered in a circle, dropping the Lefauchex, and went face-foremost to the basement's floor.

'She tried to kill me!' Belle gasped, standing with the smoking Dance dangling at her side.

'That's what she must've been getting at when she kept asking me if I'd side her against everybody, even you, "Brother Ed",' Waco growled. 'She aimed to do it all along.'

'Looks that way,' Dusty answered. 'Only this's one hell of a time to discuss it. Let's go. That crowd will be so riled they'll not stop to ask us what's happened, or why we did it.'

Holstering her Dance, Belle joined the men in the

rush to the stairs and out of the building. They ran to the waiting horses, set free the reins and swung into the saddles.

'What do we do?' yelped Dunco, looking thoroughly shaken and scared.

'Scatter and ride like hell!' Dusty advised. 'Go in twos at the most. Come on, Mellie-gal!'

'Which's the way to the ranch?' Downend demanded.

'Out to the northwest, happen that's where you want to go,' Dusty answered. 'We aim to head *anyplace* except there.'

'He's right, Miller!' Dunco stated, watching Dusty and Belle send their horses in a different direction to that selected by the Kid and Waco. 'Let's go south to Mexico. This deal's gone way too far for safety.'

Walking towards the theatre, Corbeau, Kincaid, Raphael, Mick and the other nine men looked every inch a U.S. Cavalry captain, his sergeant and troopers. A closer examination would have revealed that their tunics bore the buttons of a long defunct Kansas regiment of Dragoons. Under the circumstances, however, nobody would be likely to have been so observant. Corbeau's party would have been larger, but there were neither extra uniforms, nor more men sufficiently fanatical to the Cause to be entrusted with such a delicate mission.

Everything was still highly chaotic outside the building, although not so bad as it had been a few minutes earlier. Already the marshal had departed, taking the majority of the audience's male members to form a posse and 'hunt down' the assassins. Claiming—loudly so as to be heard by as many people as possible—that he intended to bring in living prisoners, the peace officer had declined the ranchers' and foremens' offers of assistance.

Pierce and the other 'survivors' stood in an apparently disconsolate group, clear of the remnants of

the audience. Not far away, a Rocker ambulance* was
parked before the theatre's main entrance, its rear doors
thrown open. Dripping blood in a convincing manner—from bottles they held beneath the blankets which
concealed them—three motionless shapes on stretchers
were carried out of the building. Low mutters of sympathy, or deep anger, rose at the sight. Hats were swept
from heads and anger showed on many faces.

Watching the crowd's reaction, Corbeau felt certain
that de Richelieu's scheme would be successful. Even if
open war with the Yankees did not immediately result,
the flames they had kindled that night in San Antonio
de Bexar would smoulder and grow until the South rose
again.

The appearance of the 'soldiers' created something of
a stir, drawing attention from the departing ambulance.
Stalking forward, sabre held in the regulation manner as
it dangled sheathed on his weapon belt's slings. Corbeau
halted his men. Apart from the buttons, everything
looked just right. Kincaid, with a sergeant's chevrons on
his sleeves, toted a revolver in the traditional close-
topped Cavalry holster. Although the rest of the party
also displayed holstered sidearms they each had a
Springfield single-shot carbine hanging by its sling at
their right sides.† While the men had wished to carry
either *Chassepot* or Henry rifles, Dusty Fog had pointed
out that they would lose credibility by doing so. Having
a few Springfield carbines, de Richelieu had overruled
their objections and insisted that the single-shot
weapons were taken.

The small Texan had tried to visualize every eventuality and eliminate, as far as possible, the danger to
his friends. While not gunfighters in the accepted sense
of the word, Shanghai Pierce, Miffin Kennedy and
Richard King could take care of themselves in a

* A description of a Rocker ambulance is given in: *HOUND DOG
MAN*.

† A description of the functions of a carbine-sling is given in: *GO
BACK TO HELL*.

dangerous situation. Knowing that they would most probably be outnumbered, Dusty had tried to even out the odds.

'Gentlemen,' Corbeau greeted, addressing the ranchers in a well-simulated Northern accent.

'What the——?' Shanghai Pierce growled, looking startled. 'Where did you blue-bellies come from?'

'We learned of a plot to assassinate the Governor and the members of the peace conference,' Corbeau explained. 'So I was ordered to come here and protect——.'

'You left it a mite late for that,' slim, wiry Richard King declared, sounding genuinely bitter.

'Y—you mean——?' Corbeau gasped, acting just as well as any of the ranchers' party, as he swung and stared after the departing Rocker ambulance.

'You didn't come fast enough,' the tall, tanned, well-built Miffin Kennedy pointed out.

'No, sir, but we tried,' Corbeau answered. 'My orders were to take everybody concerned with the conference under my protection.'

'*Protection!*' Kennedy barked, slapping at where his revolver should have been hanging at his right thigh. 'My old hawg-leg's the only protection——.'

The words trailed off as the rancher's face registered his realization that he was unarmed. Fortunately all three men, while not actors, were skilled in the business of horse-trading. So they possessed sufficient histrionic ability to fool their opponents in the deadly game.

'You said, Mr. Kennedy?' Corbeau challenged; a typical rank-conscious senior officer who had made his point with an influential citizen and placed the other at a disadvantage.

'All right, so none of us are dressed,' Kennedy growled, glancing at the unadorned thighs of his companions. 'Maybe we'd best do what the captain says.'

Corbeau also raked the party with his eyes. For such an important social engagement, they had donned their best town clothes and none sported the gunbelt with which he normally counted himself as being fully dressed. Young Counter had achieved that most important part of the plan.

Thinking of the blond giant's success brought another point to Corbeau's attention.

'Who were the victims, gentlemen?'

'The Governor, Dusty Fog and Mark Counter,' Pierce replied. 'Hey! It wasn't me who hired those two yahoos who killed them.'

'Or me!' Kennedy asserted.

'I'm damned if *I* did!' King went on heatedly. 'I figured we'd won——.'

Suddenly Corbeau realized in which direction the conversation was drifting. He had only half heard the first two protestations of innocence, being engrossed in his own thoughts. Learning that Mark Counter had been a 'victim' had momentarily thrown him off balance. Then he had understood. That was why the Baroness de Vautour had been cultivating the acquaintance of young 'Caxton'. She had always hated the blond giant, for some reason, and had taken her revenge regardless of how doing it might affect the rest of their plans.

'Who was responsible isn't our concern at the moment, gentlemen,' Corbeau interrupted, not wanting the crowd to think too closely upon that aspect. 'Our informant said that you are all to be killed. So I intend to escort you to a place of safety.'

'What if we allow we're safe enough, way we are?' Pierce inquired.

'I have my orders, sir,' Corbeau replied, pleased that the opportunity to do so had arisen. 'I have to take you, regardless of how you feel on it.'

'And if we don't go?' Kennedy asked.

'I *have* my orders, gentlemen,' Corbeau insisted, 'Under the circumstances, I would be compelled to enforce them.'

'You mean take us against our will?' King wanted to know.

'If I have to,' Corbeau agreed. 'My orders come from the highest authority.'

'Best do like he says, boys,' Pierce advised. 'Damn it all. I feel right naked without my plough-handle.'

'We have horses at the Charro livery barn,' Corbeau announced. 'Mounts for you gentlemen are available there. It will save us time in getting you to a place of safety.'

'You're bossing this trail drive,' King declared and the others gave their muttered agreement.

Already the crowd was scattering. The few who had shown signs of being interested in the ranchers and soldiers were persuaded to go about their business. That had been handled by Kincaid, acting in a tough, bullying manner calculated to arouse bitterness and remain in the recipients' minds. Without actually using violence, as he had urged the onlookers to get the hell to their homes, he had conveyed a suggestion that he would very much like to. Certainly there had been many hostile glances and muttered comments about 'damned Yankee blue-bellies' by the time he had completed his work.

There was little conversation as the men walked through the streets. As they passed along an alley towards the Charro livery barn, the soldiers slipped the rings of their carbines free from the slings' clips. They held the weapons in both hands before them, but did not yet elevate the barrels into a firing position.

Although the barn's main doors were wide open, and its interior illuminated by lamps, there was no sign of its owner and his employees. The latter had been sent to a saloon and given sufficient money by Corbeau to ensure that they did not return in a hurry, while the former had been a guest at the theatre. Corbeau's party had left their horses, ready for a hurried departure, fastened to the top rail of the nearest corral.

'Your mounts are inside, gentlemen,' Corbeau remarked, his voice showing a tinge of tension. 'If you'll collect them, we'll move out.'

Allowing the ranchers' party to draw ahead, the 'soldiers' followed them into the barn. It had been decided that the shooting should be done where there would be no chance of survivors escaping into the darkness. If Corbeau and his men had been less confident and more observant, they might have seen that their victims were striding out at a faster pace and putting distance between them.

On entering the building, the 'soldiers' fanned out to form a line. In its center, Corbeau and Kincaid started to draw their revolvers. The former had changed his weapon, producing an 1860 Army Colt instead of the Webley with which he had saved Mark Counter's life.

Something moved in a shadowy corner at the right side and rear of the barn, taking shape as a giant of a man.

Another, smaller figure emerged from the unlit proprietor's office to the left of the room.

Up in the hayloft, a female and two male figures rose from places of concealment behind the bales of hay.

Flickering his gaze around, Corbeau felt as if an icy finger had rubbed itself along his spine.

Mark Counter moved into the lighted area, uninjured, with his jacket removed and the *buscadero* gunbelt strapped on.

Stepping forward, 'Ed Caxton' halted with hands raised ready to go into sudden, devastating action.

Up in the loft, 'Matt Caxton' stood, with his hands thumb-hooked into his gunbelt, at 'Melanie Beauchampaine's' right side. Winchester rifle dangling with deceptive negligence in his grasp, and his face the cold, savage mask of a *Pehnane* Dog Soldier, 'Alvin "Comanche" Blood' conveyed the impression of a mountain lion crouching to spring from the girl's left.

Shaken by the sudden interruption to their arrangements, Corbeau's party froze into immobility.

Turning fast, the ranchers and their foremen sent hands dipping inside jackets to the weapons they had carried concealed but ready for use.

'Get them!' Corbeau screamed, lifting his Colt.

All hell tore loose in the barn!

Out flickered Dusty's, Mark's and Waco's Colts; in that order. Three double crashes shattered the brief hush which had followed Corbeau's words, being echoed by the rapid blasting of the Winchester which had flowed lightning fast to the Kid's shoulder. Then a variety of short-barreled, easily-hidden revolvers banged, cracked, or spat, in the hands of the would-be victims.

Faced with the threat of certain death for their friends—or themselves—the Texans threw lead in the only way they dared under the circumstances.

To kill!

Corbeau went down, with Dusty Fog's first two bullets smashing apart his skull. Taking Mark's twin loads in the chest, Kincaid died an instant later. A split-second after that, Raphael fell to the long-barreled Colts in Waco's hands. This time the 'Caxton brothers' had something more lethal than wads of paper ahead of the powder charges in their revolvers' chambers.

First of his party to recover from the shock, Mick had managed to bring his carbine almost to his shoulder, before a flat-nosed Winchester bullet impaled his brain and crumpled him as limp as a disemboweled rag doll.

A veritable tempest of lead slashed its way into the ranks of the Brotherhood. Yet not one of them tried to surrender. Even when stricken, the blue-clad figures attempted to continue the fight. Before the Texans dared cease firing, every member of Corbeau's party lay dead.

The price of the slaughter, and for preventing the possibility of another civil war, had been a bloody furrow carved across Figert's side.

If it had not been for the courage of Belle Boyd, the planning ability of Dusty Fog, the horse-savvy of the Ysabel Kid and the faith of the other men in the small Texan, the cost would have been far dearer.

CHAPTER SEVENTEEN

I Owe Him My Life, Belle

Colonel Anton de Richelieu, or Major Byron Aspley, looked up as the door of his study opened.

It was mid-afternoon on the day after the incident in San Antonio de Bexar. He was expecting a messenger from Corbeau; bringing word of how things had gone. Instead of returning immediately to the ranch, Corbeau's party were to head northwest into the direction of New Braunfels, as if making for the nearest Yankee army post. On reaching the Marion River, they would enter and either go up- or downstream until locating a place at which they could emerge without leaving tracks. With that done, they would make a long circle back to the Brotherhood's headquarters.

At first glance, de Richelieu assumed that the show's party had made better time than Corbeau's messenger, or were dispensing with his services and delivering the news themselves.

Then certain worrying and contradictory factors started to imprint themselves upon de Richelieu's mind.

The 'Caxton' family came in first, the 'brothers' flanking 'Ed's wife'.

However Virginie de Vautour did not follow them.

That alone was a puzzling development. Knowing the Baroness, de Richelieu would have expected her to be in the forefront of the party; eager to claim all the credit that was to be awarded. She most certainly would not have permitted the 'Caxtons'—whom she hated as a bunch of inferior beings that refused to recognize and respect her superior status in life—to precede her.

'Melanie Beauchampaine', or 'Mrs. Caxton', was wearing a dark blue shirt, riding breeches and Hessian boots, but they were not the sensually-revealing garments in which she was to have appeared on the Variety Theatre's stage. That was not too significant a point. Knowing that they would need to travel fast after they had done their work, she could have carried more suitable attire along and changed at the first opportunity.

None of which explained Virginie's absence.

Nor suggested why Mark Counter should be bringing up the rear of the newly arrived party. The blond giant should have remained in San Antonio, learning how public sentiment was reacting and steering it along the required lines.

On top of everything, the expressions on the 'Caxtons'' and young Counter's faces warned de Richelieu that all was far from well.

'What happened?' de Richelieu demanded, coming to his feet. 'Where's the Baroness?'

'She tried to kill me at the theatre, so I shot her,' the girl he knew as 'Melanie Beauchampaine' replied.

'She's dead?' de Richelieu asked.

'Yes,' the girl replied. 'Your scheme's finished, Colonel de Richelieu. My name is Belle Boyd. I'm a member of the U.S. Secret Service.'

'*Belle Boyd!*' the man repeated the name incredulously.

'I would like you to meet Captain Dusty Fog,' Belle went on, indicating the small Texan and moving her finger to point to 'Matt Caxton'. 'And Waco, of the OD Connected.'

Black rage distorted de Richelieu's face as his eyes ran from one to the other of the young people before him. Then the expression faded and the old, disciplined mask returned.

'I see,' de Richelieu growled. 'And you're in it too, Mr. Counter?'

'I'm in it, Major Aspley,' the blond giant agreed.

'Where are my men?' de Richelieu wanted to know.

'Dead,' Dusty answered. 'Not one of them would surrender, fought to the last man.'

'God rest their souls!' de Richelieu barked, stiffening to a brace and raising his hand in a salute. 'They died for their beliefs.'

'That's one way of looking at it,' Dusty drawled. 'But there'll be no war between the North and South.'

'Won't there?' de Richelieu challenged. 'Once word of what happened gets out, the radicals and liberals up North will use it against the South. My people here will lay the blame on the Yankees——.'

'I doubt it, Colonel,' Belle said, reaching behind her. She plucked out a newspaper and tossed it onto the desk. 'This is the story that will go out.'

Even before he picked up the paper, de Richelieu saw its headlines.

OUTLAWS STRIKE AT GOVERNOR

Murderous Attempt At Variety Theatre Frustrated

Reading the story, he saw that there was no hope of turning the affair into propaganda for his cause.

First came the story of the town of Hell's existence, with hints of the control it wielded over the State's outlaw population. Its organizers, fearing Governor Stanton Howard's strong-minded campaign against the lawless elements, had tried to remove him from office. Fortunately, a warning of the proposed assassination had reached the Governor. Displaying his usual courage, he had volunteered to act as bait for the trap. Apparently some hint of his future intentions—sending Ole Devil Hardin's floating outfit to Hell to reconnoitre and prepare the way for the U.S. Cavalry to bring the nefarious community to an end—had reached the town. So Captain Fog and Mark Counter had also been targets for the assassins. Being forewarned, they had all escaped injury. The men responsible—badly wanted outlaws—the 'Caxton Brothers','Comanche Blood' and their two female accomplices—had been killed resisting arrest. The same fate had been meted out to a further bunch of owlhoots who, dressed as members of the U.S. Cavalry, had been meaning to murder the other members of the Governor's peace conference, to divert attention from the real reason for the killings at the theatre. The plot had been foiled and the Governor promised an early end would be brought to the activities of the town called Hell.

No mention of the Brotherhood For Southron Freedom.

Not a hint that could be turned into a means to arouse animosity between the North and the South.

'Your idea, Captain Fog?' de Richelieu inquired, laying down the newspaper.

'Mine, and Colonel Boyd's,' Dusty agreed.

'Ah, yes. *Colonel* Boyd,' de Richelieu drawled, turning his cold eyes to the girl. 'I could expect such brilliance from the Rebel Spy—but not that she would turn traitress to the South.'

Belle winced as if she had been lashed across the face with a riding quirt. Then her features hardened into a mask as impassive as de Richelieu's.

'I swore the oath of allegiance to the Union, Colonel. And if I'd had any respect for the Brotherhood For Southron Freedom, after you caused the destruction of the *Prairie Belle* and Jim Bludso's death, the Frenchman would have driven it out.'

'The *Frenchman*?' de Richelieu said, frowning. 'What did Victor Brandt do—Of course! Madame Lucienne must have been your friend.'

'A damned good one!' Belle confirmed. 'You say Victor *Brandt* was "the *Frenchman*"?'

That was the man she had killed in the headquarters of the Shreveport military post. An ex-officer in the United States' Army, who had been dismissed from the service for mistreating the enlisted men.

'That was a private name and joke, known only to a few of us,' Richelieu explained. 'He came from the

Alsace and was of Germanic origin. So he would never admit to being French. Some of the Brotherhood called him "the Frenchman" to annoy him. He was killed by the Army in Shreveport——.'

'I killed him, as I swore I would when I saw poor Lucienne,' Belle corrected. 'No human being could have treated another as he did her.'

'I'm not excusing him, or trying to apologize for what's been done,' de Richelieu declared. 'It was the fortunes of war. And now, Colonel Boyd, what do you plan to do with me?'

All through the conversation, Mark Counter had remained silent. In his mind's eye, he could see that day during the War when Major Aspley had saved his life. Mark's horse had been shot from under him and he lay stunned by the fall. Leaping from his mount, Aspley had held back the sabre-armed Yankee cavalrymen who had rushed the blond giant. Before they had been driven off, Aspley had lost an ear and received another wound.

'I can't let you take him in,' Mark declared. 'I owe him my life, Belle.'

'What do you suggest we do, Mark?' Belle asked.

'Let him go,' answered the big blond. 'Ask him to give his word that he'll leave the country, never return or try to make more trouble for the United States. Then Lon'll guide him across the border into Mexico.'

'Very well,' Belle said. 'That's what we'll do.'

'How about my men at the camp?' de Richelieu put in. 'I'll not leave them to face the consequences.'

'They won't suffer from it,' Mark promised. 'I'll go over and tell them that the Brotherhood's disbanded and send them to their homes.'

'Some of them won't be sorry to go, the way you've been driving them,' de Richelieu drawled. 'You've done a real fine job, Mr. Counter.'

'My thanks, sir,' Mark said, flushing a little with delight at the praise.

'The keys to my safe are in the desk's drawer,' de Richelieu went on. 'In it, you'll find the Brotherhood's funds. Use them to pay off the men.'

'We'll do that,' Dusty assured the man. 'Now, sir, about Mark's suggestion. Will you give us your word?'

'Would Colonel Boyd accept it?' de Richelieu challenged.

'Of course, because I know that you will keep it,' the girl replied. 'And apart from that, I can't have you arrested and brought to trial without the whole story coming out. *That* would never do.'

'Making such an admission to me could be a mistake, Colonel Boyd,' de Richelieu pointed out.

'You've already thought of it—and know that we, the Secret Service, daren't let you go to trial.'

'What do I do if I accept your offer?'

'Go back to Europe. A soldier of your ability can always find employment.'

'And if I decide to stay and go to trial?'

'Don't, Major Aspley, *please*,' Belle begged. 'If you try, you'll never see the inside of a court. *I'd* have to see to that.'

'You'd kill me?' de Richelieu inquired.

'I would,' the girl confirmed, scarcely louder than a whisper. 'I'd even do that, before I'd see our country plunged into another civil war.'

'I wouldn't want a lady—and a loyal Southerner—to have that on her conscience,' de Richelieu declared. 'And I give you my apologies, ma'am, for calling you a traitress. I wish I'd had a dozen like you on my side.'

'My thanks, sir,' Belle said stiffly.

'Do I have *your* word, *Colonel* Boyd,' de Richelieu continued, 'that my men will not be arrested or in any way punished? None of them at the camp have taken part in our operations.'

'You have it, sir,' Belle replied. 'They are free to go.'

'Then I give you mine,' de Richelieu barked. 'May I leave now?'

'The Ysabel Kid's got horses waiting, Major,' Dusty drawled. 'If you'll come with us?'

'Very well,' de Richelieu agreed. 'But I don't need an escort. You can rely on me to waste no time in leaving.'

'It's your choice, sir,' Dusty answered.

Making way for de Richelieu to pass, the girl and the Texans followed him from the building. The Kid was waiting outside, with two saddled horses.

'The Colonel's leaving alone, Lon,' Dusty drawled.

'Why, sure,' the Indian-dark Texan replied and handed over the reins of de Richelieu's mount.

Swinging into the saddle, de Richelieu gravely saluted Belle. Then he turned the animal and started it moving. Nobody spoke as he rode away.

Fifty yards from the building, de Richelieu dropped his right hand and thumbed open the flap of his holster. Drawing the revolver, he reined the horse around.

'The South will rise again!' he roared and set his spurs to work.

Bounding forward, the horse carried its rider back in the direction from which it had come. De Richelieu fired once, his bullet splitting the air close to Mark Counter's head.

Sliding the Winchester from its saddle boot, the Kid pivoted and flung its butt to his collarbone. He squinted along the barrel and squeezed the trigger. Smoke wafted briefly between his and the onrushing figure, but his rifleman's instincts told him that he had made a hit.

Sure enough, when the smoke cleared, the Kid saw de Richelieu sliding from the saddle.

Guns in hand, Belle and the Texans ran forward. De Richelieu sprawled on his back, mortally wounded but still alive and conscious, when they reached him.

'Why'd you do it, Major?' Mark asked, kneeling by the stricken, dying man. 'We'd let you go, knowing you'd keep your word.'

'I saved your life because it was my duty as your commanding officer,' de Richelieu replied.

'And I saved yours for doing it,' Mark pointed out.

'You owed me nothing, I merely did my duty,' de Richelieu corrected. 'If I'd taken your offer, I'd have been beholden to you, Mr. Counter. No major wants to be that to a first lieutenant.'

Two minutes later, de Richelieu was dead.

Leaving Mark to visit the camp and send the men home, Belle and Dusty watched Waco and the Kid take shovels to dig a grave.

'It's over, Belle,' Dusty said.

'Will it *ever* really be over?' the girl countered. 'Lord, I hope so. And I hope the day never comes when the South has to rise again.'